GIVE ME YOUR ANSWER

GIVE ME YOUR ANSWER

A Novel

J.K. PETRIE

Ungirl Publishing

Contents

PART TWO

*Dedicated to my sibling Anthony
and anyone else who cries over video games.*

PROLOGUE

My body reverberated with music right before it happened. And right after, the blood rushing through my ears drowned it all out, leaving only the sound of my heart beating in double-time. It throbbed with the music at first, then it fought against the beat. Just like how my existence was off-beat with the party itself. A fourth grader's recorder playing over a recording of a symphony, rehearsed and natural, truly effortless underneath my distracting attempts to pretend I could be just as on-key while the recording kept playing as if I was not there at all. I never wanted the party in the first place, but I thought that it was a kind favor from a friend. What you're *supposed* to do for your birthday. I was only a teenager, and I had a pitiful amount of life experience. Books took priority over all else and that made me vulnerable.

Of *course* I was awkward. I had few points of reference for navigating life in general, let alone college parties. For all my other birthdays, maybe I'd steal a beer from my dad's minifridge, maybe I'd sneak out and sit on top of the playground set by my house. Study what few stars I could see until I went home and dreamt about seeing them all. But this time, I was surrounded by people I didn't know, all of them celebrating. Not my eighteenth, though. All of the free booze that *he'd* provided for them with his daddy's money. He might have been just as awkward as me deep down underneath it all, but he had all of the wealth in the world to compensate for it.

I was a little suspicious that he'd done so much for me. I mean, we were friends back then, but I was still privy to his slight Machiavellian nature. I'd asked him why, and he'd replied, *Only the best for my business partner.* It made me crack a grin, and all of my doubt melted away. Which was a mistake. He really knew how to feed into my fragile ego.

There were too many people for me, and I didn't like how loud it was, either. At some point during the night, I decided to escape to the balcony. I could still feel the floor thumping, even outside. There was a complete open bar, but my fist clenched around the bottleneck of the same cheap beer I'd always liked. Kind of embarrassing to think about now. I thought I was so much better than everyone else and it showed. Likely why I didn't have any friends.

He was sitting next to me. We looked out toward the California skyline together. The only person there that I knew. We spoke. About the future of the company more than anything else, since I struggled to hang on to any other topics of conversation. How were we going to set things up? Which potential investors should we contact first? That kind of thing. It was great. We were going to build a successful future. God, things were looking up for me.

Then it all went to shit.

PART ONE

I

SECRETION

Veronica woke up on her couch in a pool of cool sweat. Voices swam around her, then became clear.

"Mutual assured destruction has proven itself to be an unsustainable, hard-and-fast strategy over the course of the past few years. For how long can politicians use it to convince the average citizen they are entirely safe from weapons built to cause destruction beyond human comprehension? I mean, let's look at the facts, okay, break it down real simple—giving one person, or an elite group of people, so much power is like handing a child a gun. Even in the United States. Now, okay, I am in no way implying that—"

"Sure, sure, maybe for you it would be like handing a child a toy gun, you can't comprehend—"

"May I finish talking?"

"No, no, I'm making a point, you can't comprehend the idea that someone else has a greater sense—"

"As I was saying—"

"of patriotism, of responsibility, especially as our leaders—"

"Excuse me. Allow one another to finish speaking. I don't like cutting mics, but I'll do it if I have to."

"Thank you. As I was saying, I am in no way implying that—that, you know, the people who have access to such weapons are necessarily any different than your average person, and more often than not, they are leagues more competent, like the leaders we have in respectable nations, right, but as a species, across the human race, there are things we cannot comprehend. It's just not the way that we are built. The same way a dog can never learn to use advanced tools or the way that—"

"Oh, oh, so we're like dogs now."

"—an ape can never learn to speak. Now, this whole thing is like a group of boys having pissing contests on a playground, and they're saying to one another, 'Oh, you have a bomb? Well, I have a nuclear, bigger, better, more destructive bomb. You have a nuclear bomb? Well, I'm going to an invent a weapon that won't only destroy everything on the planet, oh no—"

"Watch your language."

"My apologies. Anyway, it's, 'oh no, it won't just destroy everything on the planet. This is a weapon that will keep people alive through their pain. Because, you know, death is just too great of a mercy, right? And this is a weapon that was never meant to be used. But ladies and gentlemen, all across the world we have seen the effects of the Bogotá Testing Incident in Colombia, right, and the amount of immigrants who have either been left with chronic disabilities for the U.S. to take care of, no casualties, of course, that would just be too easy, and, you know, there is much reason to believe that it was an intentional attack from the Colombian government against its own citizens. Because it was a plan against the United States and its taxpayers to put us at an economic disadvantage and prime us to be attacked—because now we have these foreigners scattering up here seeking asylum and treatment for their disabilities.

And now the people who were batsh—who were crazy enough to do something like that, we know they have access to weaponry unlike what we've seen before, and what do we do as a response? We develop something just like that, but bigger, meaner, able to leave absolutely everyone on the planet disabled, mutated, sterile, and suffering until all of us die. What if the security surrounding that weapon is breached? Information leaks, ladies and gentlemen, and that is information that we are putting up for grabs merely by seeking it out, building it, discovering it. Information that these foreign nations never would have discovered had we not attempted to discover it first. It's Pandora's Box. That's how they ripped the B132 in the first place. How much intel have these shithole countries taken from us and used to create weapons none of us understand, let alone them? Should anyone have access to that info? As a matter of fact, why does the public have any knowledge of the B132 whatsoever? Just so our government can brag, have a d- I mean, flex their muscles? It's dangerous."

"Okay. For one, it's asinine to claim that we should neglect arming ourselves to keep other countries from spying. What we need is better security surrounding these projects. You're parroting far-left ideology. For two, it's unbelievable that you think that the Bogotá Testing Incident was anything more than a hoax. That happened in 2045. Decades have passed. Descendants of Colombian immigrants are still living in this country, about 50% are living off of social security, living off of

SSDI, specifically—and is there real proof of any of their disabilities? Was there ever? And if the weapon supposedly leaves you sterile, how is our country still crawling with descendants of refugees? Because it's so much easier to claim you're seeking asylum, claim disability, and live off of the hardworking taxpayers in a different, more prosperous country, right, so—"

She switched the television off.

"Fucking idiots," she whispered.

The world's political state was growing more polarized by the second ever since the billionaire died. The few people who were aware enough to notice it often failed to deduce why. It was a sore point of frustration among self-described moderates. Veronica thought she had an idea though it was not one she would ever share publicly, and it was not a *unique* idea in the first place, anyway– the mystery and shock surrounding her predecessor's disappearance created a general sense that anything was possible. People don't do well with too many possibilities. It was the perfect breeding ground for conspiracy theories of all kinds. For the bigoted, that provided an opportunity to blame whichever groups they hated the most for anything. Immigrants, mostly.

The billionaire had dipped his fingers in just about any project imaginable, meaning that almost anything could be made into a supposed hoax or secret that traced back to some conspiracy theory about the billionaire's disappearance. Most of those projects were inhumane and dismissive of the vulnerable people that were harmed because of them. People still found a way to make the billionaire the victim. Young and privileged boys followed him like he was the second coming of Jesus Christ. He was a genius, supposedly, in the scientific *and* philosophical sense. Not afraid to say what *everyone is thinking*. Didn't conform to social rules on *political correctness*.

That's how it was framed, at least.

Those fringe theorists' persecution fantasy was always there, and the billionaire's disappearance only justified it more. The public didn't know any details. Thus, rumors swirled and spread until they became mainstream. He was assassinated because he was growing too powerful. Because he was a threat to the oppressive, socialist government. Because he was just too successful– perhaps he was murdered for his money. Because he didn't conform to society's ideas on what a scientist should be. Because he spoke the truth. On women, on minorities, on the poor, immigrants, every pesky group that supposedly stops so-called respectable people from reaching their full potential. They so annoyingly demand to be treated like equals, don't they? Perhaps, they thought, he isn't even dead. Perhaps as they spoke, he was being tortured by foreigners for daring to speak out against their "shithole" and "underdeveloped" countries.

Veronica felt sick to her stomach. She attempted to clear those thoughts from her mind.

She could hardly ever watch the news anymore. Her access to so much top-secret information meant that she only grew frustrated with the inaccuracies and the bigotry. The billionaire hasn't been kidnapped by foreigners. He wasn't killed because of his belief system. Nobody involved in government secrecy had ever even considered murdering him—of course not. He upheld all of the oppressive beliefs that this supposedly "libertarian" country had enforced on its citizens for decades. He aided them in carrying out the propaganda and the surveillance tools needed to keep citizens afraid. Of hunger, homelessness, of exile, of pain and punishment. None of the noble imagery constructed around him ever truly applied. He was a monster. He died choking in a pool of his own saliva, a man so unlikeable and evil that not even his own creation could stand to keep him alive.

The rage inside of her waned momentarily. *Was she ever even really artificially created at all?*

All of her late-night anger was replaced with contemplation. Those late-night musings seemed to happen more and more each day.

Veronica hoisted herself up from the couch to make a cup of tea. She thought better of having a beer that late at night. Her toes met something furry and warm, and indignant mewling broke the quiet. She looked down at her feet. A pair of bright blue eyes stared up at her. Her cat, too, seemed to sense the change in Veronica's mood, lately. *She's gotten so demanding,* Veronica thought tiredly as she purred and circled her little slinky body around Veronica's feet, meowing again, trying to get her to follow her to the bedroom. Purrs rumbled out of her snow-white chest as she gently pushed the cat aside with her foot. "Sorry," Veronica whispered, "Not yet." She cupped her mug, trying not to let its warm steam tempt her back to sleep, and walked to her desk.

It had been about a month since she extracted the chip from Eclipta's brain. Much had happened since then. For one, Veronica inherited the billionaire's company. Surprising, really. Especially after she'd been fired so soon prior. Perhaps he'd never thought to change his will, but even then, Veronica was surprised she was in it at all. Especially with no conditions regarding her employment. It was black and white, entirely perplexing in its simplicity– she was to inherit the company in the event of his death or disappearance. That's it. No strings. It felt unreal. She supposed that she always thought that...the company would sort of die with him. He and his corporation were synonymous with one another. There was no line between where he ended and the business side of his life began. Actually, that was something he'd said very plainly in the past during interviews when asked how he balanced his personal life and his business life. "I don't differentiate the two," he'd say flatly. "My business is my life. My life is my business. It's perfect that way."

He had no heirs, no surviving family that he knew of, and Veronica was the closest thing to a second-in-command that he ever had. Which was sad, given how he treated her. Maybe he genuinely had no other options, even if he did look over his will again after he fired her.

The downside to inheriting his company was that Veronica was catapulted into the public spotlight like never before. She didn't know how long she'd be able to stomach the conspiracy theories. They sprouted just as soon as she stepped up to take his place. There was some good to being treated like just another lowly worker back when she was the head engineer. Nobody paid attention to her.

She *hated* attention.

Veronica was only reassured by her confidence in the fact that she had security protecting her secrets that nobody would manage to ever override. They certainly attempted, though.

People thought that she may have had a hand in the billionaire's disappearance. She frowned. Veronica was incredibly lucky that he'd covered for her after she stole the Alien Girl. He kept it hush-hush enough that it was not information that anyone would be able to access– really, there was no record of it happening what-soever. Impressive, considering just how surveilled everything became in recent years. The billionaire framed it to the police as a complete misunderstanding. A miscommunication between Alien Girl's transport and himself. "They accidentally triggered her security system," he'd told them. "This is a company issue, not a legal matter. Thank you." They bought it.

Of course, the only reason he decided to cover for her was so he could keep the Alien Girl's...*humanity*...as secret as possible. She shuddered at the idea that she had not *stolen* a secret project of the billionaire's; really, she had *kidnapped* a sentient being. Either way, if a secret like that leaked to the public...it would be bad, to say the least.

"There's really no point in worrying about it," she whispered. Despite all the power her newfound position provided her, she hadn't been taking advantage of it, really. She only used it for access to more secrets. The ultimate insider information. All of the company's gears were perfectly in place already, a fine-tuned conglomerate machine that functioned just fine without much input. Oiled with the blood, sweat, and tears of the proles. A pang of guilt pierced her stomach and she frowned. Now she was at the top. A regular *American success story*. How terrible.

She knew that the billionaire was little more than a self-important figurehead, of course, but she was still surprised that the position he held was just as easy as she always imagined.

Easier, even. All of the conferences he attended, public meetings, seminars, the instructions he barked at his workers, they were all utterly unnecessary. It was yet another way for him to stroke his own ego and fuel his selfish pet projects.

An image of the billionaire smothered with a pink-stained dirty pillow flashed in Veronica's mind, burnt to the back of her brain.

He's not there anymore. He's burnt to ashes.

That thought was more comforting than it should have been.

Alien Girl doesn't exist anymore either.

That thought was oddly comforting, too. She stared at the chip in her hand. She wasn't dead, not alive. Nothing at all. No need to worry about someone who doesn't exist.

The comfort of those two traces of the billionaire's death helped her fall back asleep that night.

2

RED

The sun dappled in through Veronica's window, skimming her skin to a glowing orange and turning the backs of her eyelids a painful red. Half-asleep, she elected to ignore it until she was forced to awake by the distant sound of her phone ringing. She groaned and wrapped her legs around her cat-shaped pillow, pulling it closer toward her body. *It can't even be six yet,* she thought bitterly. She was tempted to blame her exhaustion on the sun's early arrival, but really, she struggled to sleep almost every single night regardless of the time of year. Stress dreams plagued her so she could not even escape the world in her sleep. The wrinkles on her face deepened by the day with no regard for the fact that she was still in her twenties.

Veronica could not understand how the billionaire coped so well with the limelight, the persecution, the political tension of it all. *It takes a sociopath.* She pinched the bridge of her nose. If she had to guess, he probably didn't dream at all when he slept. The man acted as if he'd never had a nightmare in his entire life. And what *good* dreams were there for him to have? Dreams of women, of money? Success? He had that at his fingertips in the waking world. Aside from that, it was difficult to imagine him as a man who had enough personhood in him to have any dreams at all. Meanwhile, she was haunted. No thanks to him.

He pervaded her thoughts constantly. Took up real estate that could have been used for far more productive purposes. Like emotional intelligence. Public image. More tech ideas.

She trudged across the house to pick up her cell. She cringed when she saw the screen. *Almost dead. Forgot to charge it.* She pressed it up to her ear. "Veronica speaking," she said, trying to make herself sound as awake as possible.

"Hey," a voice on the other end responded. Her executive assistant, Josiah. "Public appearance today, right? We remember? Yeah?"

His tone was always chipper, almost a little *too* casual for her liking, when they weren't executing a private operation together. It struck her that they'd need to have another one again. He was one of the few people that she trusted enough to keep near.

Since inheriting the company, Veronica lived under constant scrutiny and suspicion. Try as she might, she was nowhere near as personable as the billionaire was, even *if* her status helped in some cases. Likeability, Veronica had learned from him, could trump all circumstance, no matter the caliber. She was never sociable, never cool, never especially attractive, and there was not a single charming bone in her body. Throwing conspiracy theories about homicide and treason into the mix did not help.

As far as everyone knew, the billionaire was missing. According to the court of public opinion, Veronica was a prime suspect. Regardless, there was no way for anyone to implicate her in any way. For then.

That didn't stop people from developing ideas. Not with Veronica's background, and especially not with all of the potential motivation she had to kill him. *Lots* of people had plenty of motivation to kill him, but unluckily for her, she was the easiest suspect.

I mean, I did always think I'd be the one to do it, she thought. She almost laughed out loud. *Wow. I can't believe I'm actually innocent.*

Josiah's tone became more aggressively cheerful as it crackled through the speaker, irritation seeping into his smiley voice. "Veronica? Hello? Interview?"

Oh. Interview.

"Interview?" Veronica repeated, sounding more unsure than she meant.

"Interview," Josiah confirmed.

She fell silent. Josiah sighed.

"Be there to pick you up in an hour." He hung up.

"Shit," she whispered.

—

"Did you brush your teeth?" Josiah asked. Veronica had just sprinted down the steps of her apartment, all but flying into the back of his car.

"Yeah," she responded between shallow pants.

"With something other than beer?"

She shot him a look. "Are you going to smell my breath to check, *Dad?*"

He gave her a giant smile in the rearview mirror. She sighed, only partly in an attempt to finish catching her breath.

As he started driving, Veronica checked over herself. She didn't look in a mirror before leaving. Her suit was straight, or at least it seemed to be– hard to tell from that angle. She'd put on a little cologne before leaving. Her hair was fine. Nothing was wrinkled, save for the small lines framing her face a little too soon for comfort. She'd moisturized her skin, but she wasn't sure if it would do anything for her eyebags. She'd probably look tired either way. Not out of the norm, at least.

After a few miles of silence, only filled with the weirdly awkward sound of the car's scolding tongue-click turn signal, Josiah spoke again. "You worry me," he stated. His tone was matter-of-fact.

"Huh?"

"You worry me." He took a deep breath. "Veronica, you're obsessed."

"With who?"

"You know who."

Her mouth turned into a thin straight line. "Mm."

"You're obsessed, yet you never told us what really happened. Just that he's dead. What's up with that?"

"Watch what you say. You never know who's listening," Veronica responded dryly.

Josiah paused. "We were willing to die for this. Some of us *did* die for this."

Veronica cringed.

"This is what you said you wanted," he continued, whispering, "but now I'm not so sure."

"I'm happy. This is exactly the kind of outcome I hoped for. What the world needed. What *I* needed. I got my closure," she snapped. "You've forgotten your place."

Quiet filled the car once more. Veronica began picking little blue-gray threads out of the fabric of her pants. She didn't care if they got ruined. She didn't care about anything, right then.

They finally pulled into the parking lot.

—

She vaguely remembered how she was meant to answer every question, but she was not as prepared as she would have liked. She knew that they wouldn't be particularly hard or thoughtful questions, anyway. Her publicist was pickier about where she would appear these days, so she intentionally chose a program that was well-known for being fairly milquetoast and family-friendly. It was a long-running show, and she remembered her teachers showing it in class to teach them about famous inventors and important world leaders. To *inspire* their group of bored grade schoolers. Scandals and controversies were simply not something that they ever included. Veronica imagined herself projected onto a classroom's whiteboard, another talking head among the sea of people that seemed almost mythical to her when she was in grade school. It was difficult to comprehend. Maybe her publicist was turning her attention to making her look good to the youth, considering what so many adults thought of Veronica. They were more impressionable and easy to mold, after all, and the nostalgia factor could be used to gain their favor when they got older. And wasn't she the one who insisted on trying to get Axis t-shirts back in style again? *Do teens still like tie-dye?* she'd asked.

Veronica smirked and shut her eyes. She was surrounded by glaring, cold lights, and they felt like they were burning into her retinas. Her lack of sleep didn't help. Her stomach hurt– all she'd had that day was a black coffee. She watched colors and static swirl in and out of her vision, listened to the low professional voices around her. She focused on the feeling of makeup brushes on her face.

It may have been a calloused way to think of it, but she couldn't help but feel entirely hopeless about her image. Frankly, she just wanted to get it over with.

Her interviewer, a blonde woman who looked to be in her fifties, was sitting a few feet across from her in a folding chair. She hadn't said a word to Veronica since their brief introduction and handshake. Veronica subtly side-eyed her. Her eyes were rolled back in her head as a makeup artist applied eyeliner to her waterline, her hair gently tousled over her shoulders. Even from that distance, she could smell her interviewer's perfume, expensive and too-strong, matching her commanding presence. Yet she was behaving as if Veronica was not there at all. It was a little strange. *Maybe that's just her sense of professionalism,* Veronica thought. *Maybe she's too wrapped up in other things.* She *had* been taking calls and responding to texts (Veronica knew because of how loud the tapping sounds on her cell phone were) on top of getting her makeup done, so perhaps she truly was just too busy to talk. Veronica sympathized. She knew that she could be the exact same way.

It all began before she knew it. Veronica straightened her back, checking her hair to make sure nothing was out of place one last time. She wasn't very good at smiling. She didn't do it often. Still, she forced one when her interviewer finally acknowledged her presence and shook her hand– on-screen, this time.

"Veronica," her interviewer started, "Former head engineer of Axis, now made into its chief executive officer. In your twenties, no less! Now, tell me, how does that feel?"

"Well," Veronica replied, "it's an honor, really. I've been provided many opportunities throughout my journey with Axis. I hope to continue to provide those same opportunities to others, as well. And, you know, it isn't exactly easy work. But it's still worth it."

"I'm sure it's easier for you than most." The interviewer's tone had no warmth behind it. She seemed like she was in the same boat as Veronica– just wanted to get it all over with. "You know, I think that I speak for everybody in the country when I say that his disappearance has had a monumental impact on all of us."

Monumental, Veronica thought. *Throwing in those elementary vocabulary words for the young'uns.*

"I'd like to hear more about your relationship with him. How you met him. We know that he was somewhat of a mentor to you. How is this affecting you?" She continued.

Veronica took extra care to keep her gaze steady. She attempted to add a tinge of sadness to her eyes, somehow. She wasn't a good actress. "Well," she said, "I met him in college. We both were accepted into Yale's STEM OnTrack program. It was...a pretty big deal to me, I have to say. My family doesn't come from money, and I got to go to it full-ride. It was the opportunity of a lifetime, and I was absolutely going to take it. We were among the first to enroll in the program. It was brand-new at the time.

I was the youngest among my cohorts, thirteen years old. He was seventeen. I barely got in, seeing how it was a program meant for 'high school-aged students.' But, you know, my science teacher encouraged me to advocate for myself using the fact that I *was* in high school at the time...I just wasn't what you'd think of as *high school-aged.*" She let out a nervous chuckle. *Stop over-explaining, moron.* She cleared her throat and continued speaking.

"So I guess you could say that our mentor and student-like relationship started there, considering that he was so much older than me. I can't lie, we were...kind of rivals, too. But we grew to respect one another, and that's around the time we began conceptualizing Axis. It's so strange to run the company without him here...I mean, I'm used to being the one behind the scenes. Not in front of a camera like this." She gestured toward it. She noticed a quirk in the interviewer's expression. Her stomach flipped. She began to backtrack. "And I liked working behind the scenes, you know. But what I need to do right now is advocate for him until he's found and returns home. He's not...the only team member I've ever lost. I need to do right by the company for everyone who can't anymore."

The interviewer took a moment to soak in all of the information. "Wow," she said, "That was...a lot. Thank you for sharing. I'd like to loop back to something you said earlier. You mentioned that your family didn't come from money. What was your home life like?"

Veronica's gut turned. *Out of all the things I said, why is this what we're focusing on? This wasn't in the script.*

"Well. It's not something I talk about that often." She remembered the target audience for this program– middle America and middle *schoolers*– and paused. *Maybe she's fishing for inspiration porn.* "*Anyone can do it,*" something like that. "But I was just, like, your average kid. My dad lost his job for a while. We had to live off of his savings. It wasn't always easy, but he made sure I was fed and clothed. Happy enough overall, you know? I'm not going to lie and say that luck wasn't involved at all, but most of it was hard work to get into that program and give myself a head start in life."

"And what about your mother?" the interviewer said.

Veronica froze. *What is she getting at?*

"My mother died when I was five," Veronica said. "I don't...really remember her."

The interviewer had no reaction to that information. "Where was she from?"

"She was from France."

"No, Veronica. *Where was she from?*"

"She...was born and raised in France. I'm not sure what you m-"

"I mean, your mother's family was not originally from France. She was a second-generation immigrant, correct? What culture did they claim before then?"

Veronica glanced over at the crew filming them. They were whispering to one another. Was that out of the norm? Were they as nervous as she was?

"My mother's parents were from Colombia," she said flatly. "But I never met my mother's family. I know nothing about them."

"So I suppose you don't know anything about the Bogotá Testing Incident, either?" Her tone was low and dark. She was leaning forward and coldly staring straight through Veronica. "Nothing about the secrecy behind that? The advantages it's given *you*? What about *your* secrets, Veronica? Got skeletons in *your* closet?"

Veronica froze, her vision swimming in rage and confusion. *"Cut the cameras!"* someone shouted. Her interviewer said something about censorship, pointing at Veronica with shaking accusation and rage. Her eyes were fiery and self-righteous. Like she was living out some kind of long-lived persecution fantasy right at that very moment. She looked close and far away at the same time, wading in and out of her vision. She felt a hand on her shoulder. Veronica looked up dully.

"C'mon," Josiah said. "Let's go."

ROLES

"She's peaked already, anyway," Josiah said. "She's probably not even right in the head anymore. I don't know, maybe she snorted a line before the interview, or something. Like, she's been getting more obviously right-wing, right? Just look at who she's following on Twitter! She's a nut. Everyone *knows* she's a nut, she's just out and proved their point now."

Veronica stared out the window blankly, thankful for the dark tint. She was sure that people were hoping to get a photo of her post-interview. "Not everyone."

"Veronica. They're just..." Josiah paused. "A...a vocal minority, you know? Most people are just *fine* with you. And, you know, there's no way she's going to keep that job for much longer. She's probably been fired already. You get me?"

Veronica thought about the one word she could make out from the woman's lips, her face blurry behind her accusing crimson-polished fingertip. *Censorship.* "Maybe not *that* job, no," she muttered. It was dreary and wet outside. She watched the rain-doused palm trees sway in the wind, the lights reflect off of the streets, blending together into a sickly rainbow.

"And I mean, who's going to side with a woman who brought up your m-" Josiah stopped himself like he was choking on his words. Mumbling, he continued, "Who brought up the things she did, I mean." She did not respond.

The car filled with silence. She didn't even say goodbye when she got out and trudged her way back up the apartment's steps.

—

Rage-laden sobs and screams erupted into her pillow. *I fucking hate this world, fucking hate this world. I fucking HATE this world.*
All because of HIM.

She hated that she had to pretend like he was a good person at all during her interview. She hated that regardless of how she answered people's questions, she could never win. Before she turned off her phone, her lock screen was a stream of endless notifications, all of them posts and messages about the show. She couldn't stomach looking at it. Certain phrases still circled their way through her head like a swarm of wasps.

Cocky, bragging, overconfident, fake, ungrateful, got put in her place, bad childhood, not raised right, killer, killer, killer, illegal. Alien.

She was tempted to peel herself off the mattress and smash her phone with a hammer. But for then, all she could do was screech until her throat was hoarse, then silently cry until she fell asleep.

—

The sun was setting when she woke up again. The melancholy

feeling in her stomach worsened with the golden sunlight filtering into her dark bedroom. Birds sang lowly. She was reminded of how it felt to take a nap after a hard day at school. A strange breed of nostalgia dropped itself into the bottom of her gut.

The plushies residing in the net hung against the corner of her room lordly watched over her. Her cat pillow, an orange tabby, was smudged brown. Veronica felt dim confusion before she remembered the foundation they applied before her interview. She was too drained to feel annoyed with the fact she'd have to clean it later. She rubbed her eyes and turned on the crescent moon-shaped LED lights hanging from her ceiling. Her throat burned. Her eyes felt puffy. She chugged a cup of water she left on her nightstand days ago and cringed at the dusty film it had collected.

Her mind sleepily regathered everything that happened earlier that day, and all of the leftover peace from her depression nap dissipated. *Back to reality,* she thought with misery.

She chose not to turn her phone back on. Nor any other internet or satellite-connected device, for that matter. She wouldn't be able to handle seeing her own interview rehashed, perverted, twisted to fit the ideology of whatever commentator chose to report on it, and God knows what else…the mere thought of it made her stomach twist into knots. She considered clearing her calendar for the next couple of days to recuperate.

Playing a game sounded good. Veronica slipped out of bed and walked into the living room. As soon as her cat realized she was awake, sweet bell-like meows broke through the apartment's quiet. Something furry pressed against her calf.

"*Brattyyyy*," Veronica whispered under her breath in a sing-song tone. "Hi, baby girl. You must be a hungry kitty."

She filled the cat's bowl with kibble and mused to herself. *At least Bratty isn't concerned with anything more than being fed on time. She has no idea that my little world is falling apart.* She sighed.

Veronica disconnected the ethernet cable from her computer and inserted a disc. It was an old JRPG she liked to play when she was young. As much as she usually enjoyed escaping into old memories, her eyes couldn't help but wander underneath her computer's monitor to stare at the case she'd been housing Alien Girl's chip in. *Daisy,* she thought to herself. *Maybe her name's Daisy? Was "Eclipta" a code name? Or just the body's name?*

She looked back at her screen in deep thought. *Does the chip have technology I could use for myself? Something I could repurpose for public use?*

She stopped herself. It wasn't right to think that way. It was capitalistic, selfish, and she could not bring back another reminder of him. She'd had enough of the billionaire for one lifetime.

...Is it selfish not to bring her back?

The thought never occurred to her before. She sort of thought about the chip as if it were an egg– only alive after it hatches, and only has the potential for life at all if it is incubated inside of a computer that can run it. On second thought, she realized that it was entirely possible that Alien Girl was...conscious, somehow. According to the laws of physics, so long as there was nothing to read the chip, there was no way that Alien Girl still existed at all. According to the laws of physics, however, there was also no way that Alien Girl could hold the same type of sentience that humans have. But was that really a "law of physics?"

We can't define sentience that simply...or at all.

Veronica pinched the cross pendant hanging from her neck and rubbed it between her forefinger and her thumb, lost in thought. Of all of the advancements humans made all the way up to that point in history, nobody ever came close to discovering what sentience actually is or where it comes from. Or what happens after people stop being sentient. If they ever do. Nothingness was still impossible for anyone to conceptualize, and perhaps it was because it doesn't actually exist. *Does she experience nothingness? Is she somewhere else entirely? Maybe even in something like an afterlife?*

The corner of her mouth twitched. Thinking about those things forced her to also reckon with her own mortality.

A grim jingle crackled out of the computer's speakers. Her eyes flashed back to the screen. She was distracted for too long and she'd lost a battle; "YOU DIED", the screen read.

4

CONNECT

The next morning was stormy and humid, just like the morning before. A sour aroma with notes of dirty nickels, wet scrambled eggs, and chlorophyll permeated through the streets of Los Angeles. Nancy breathed it in deeply and grinned. She missed this city. Since she'd been fired, she moved back in with her family to the United States. To say that it was deeply embarrassing to come back home with her tail between her legs would have been an understatement. Her mother always said that her mouth would get her in trouble one of these days, and Nancy always wrote her off– she *hated* that she was right. She'd signed an NDA, so she couldn't tell her mother exactly why she was fired. Her judgmental looks, however, made Nancy figure that she had an idea.

Needless to say, she was shocked when she received a letter from the new CEO of Axis. She was even more surprised to find that it was an invitation to return to the company. Perhaps Veronica had made a point to reach out to all of the staff the billionaire fired right before his disappearance. If that was the case, was Veronica validating the idea that maybe the billionaire wasn't in his right mind before then? After all, Nancy was not a particularly special employee, and it couldn't have been because of heat from the government. Any labor law that would have covered unfair termination no longer existed in California.

And it wasn't like Nancy personally knew her. She was a programmer while Veronica spearheaded the engineering department. They corresponded professionally through email a few times, and she saw Veronica up-close in person twice at most. A very reclusive woman. *A reclusive woman who's on my side,* Nancy thought cheerfully as she stepped out of the airport. Then she remembered that although she was returning to the same company she worked for before, she didn't actually know much about the person that would interview her. A fresh wave of anxiety washed over her momentarily, but it waned soon after. *Then again,* she thought, *I really must be a serious candidate for the company to pay for my plane ticket. The interview might just be a formality.*

After she settled herself into the back of her ride, she pulled her passport out of her pocket and stared at the stamp inside it. "The Republic of California," it read. She grinned ear-to-ear. *Wow. It's so good to be back.*

—

"Thank you, Josiah," Veronica muttered as he placed a steaming mug of coffee in front of her. It was filled with cream and sugar, just the way she liked it. She usually didn't have time to do more than brew plain coffee, so the gesture was appreciated.

"Nancy Ullman's coming in for her interview in twenty minutes," he responded.

She grunted and took a long sip of her drink, staring at her screen. She carelessly scrolled through the endless unread emails in her inbox to make herself look busy until he left the room.

As soon as the door shut behind him, she toed open the minifridge underneath her desk and took out a can of beer. She slowly lifted the tab and smothered it with her sweater in an attempt to muffle its sound as much as possible, then chugged half of it. She let out a breath of satisfaction and poured the rest of it into a different mug. "Fuck," she whispered under her breath, then chuckled. She was glad of the mints she'd brought with her that day to mask the yeasty smell on her breath later.

She still hadn't turned on her cell phone since the interview. She only kept her work phone nearby. Even then, she preferred to correspond over email or in person as much as possible. Mostly in person. Regardless of how innocuous her interactions over the internet were, her mistrust of technology–and people–was not only ever-present, but worsened as of late. *I wonder if I could implement a streamlined communications system for Axis. One that limits insecure interactions between employees as much as possible. Like a closed system that does not connect to the internet, or more in-person meetings, or–*

There was a knock at her door. Josiah's knock. She popped a mint in her mouth and placed the mug of beer beneath her desk. "Come in," she said, secretly frustrated that her train of thought (and her drinking time) was interrupted.

"Veronica, this is Miss Ullman." Josiah led a rather young looking blonde woman into her office. The first thing Veronica noticed was how many freckles peppered her pale body. The second thing was the expression of sheer wonder painted on her round face like a child at a theme park. She stopped herself from cracking a grin. *Hasn't she worked here before? It's not like she's seeing everything for the first time.*

"Thank you for escorting her, Josiah," she responded. "I can take it from here." He nodded and shut the door behind him.

"So great to meet you, Miss Ullman." Veronica extended her hand.

The woman took it. The young blonde's hands were flimsy and noodle-like. "You can call me Nancy," she said. Sheepishly, she added, "And I believe we've met before."

"Ah. My mistake," Veronica responded under her breath, feeling embarrassed. "I just. See a lot of people." She cleared her throat. "Anyways, Nancy, I'm going to go ahead and address the elephant in the room. I understand that you were terminated from Axis before. I also understand that you were terminated without reason. Without divulging too much information, I'm aware of the fact that there were...certain circumstances that may have affected your prior employer's judgment. I'd like to make that right. That being said–"

"But I *was* given a reason for termination," she blurted.

Veronica paused for a moment and blinked. "I'm sorry?" she replied. She sensed a tinge of shame in Nancy's expression as she looked down at the floor.

"I had a reason for termination," she repeated.

Veronica looked down and skimmed Nancy's documents without a word. "Nancy," she said, "Underneath your reason for termination, it clearly says 'none given.' On the papers *I* have, at least. What do you mean you had a reason to be terminated? What was it?"

She clapped her hands together. "Well," she started, "to tell you the truth–and I would *never* repeat this mistake again were I to be brought back on board, I promise–it was for disrespect."

"Insubordination?"

"Um...not really," she replied. "And it wasn't on purpose. I was told that it was for...being disrespectful to the Alien Girl? You know, the project?"

Veronica's eyes fluttered in shock. "And who told you that?" she whispered.

"The...CEO?" Nancy said softly. Her face was bright red, which especially accentuated her youthful demeanor.

"The CEO," Veronica repeated quietly.

Thick silence filled the room for a little while. Nancy shuffled uncomfortably as she paced the room, then sat back down in her big leather chair. She sighed, pulled her mug out from underneath her desk, and took a long sip from it.

"You got a favorite lunch spot?" Veronica asked.

—

"I don't know," Nancy continued, finishing her story. "I guess I just freaked out. Something about her seemed so...*real*." Veronica noticed that she'd been dipping the same tortilla chip into the bowl of queso between them for at least two minutes. Nancy struggled to make eye contact with her for longer than a couple of seconds at a time, constantly flashing her focus between Veronica's gaze and her own lap. "I know that's stupid."

"Sentience is subjective," Veronica replied. "Maybe things

gain sentience when we give them power. Like tulpas..." She trailed off.

"What?"

It was Veronica's turn to be embarrassed. "Nevermind. It's...a Tibetan Buddhist thing that the internet made into something...different." She didn't like revealing just how *logged on* she was in her conversations with other people. It made her feel pathetic. "My point is that it's not strange that she unnerved you. Nothing really distinguished her from a real person."

"I guess that I just don't see it the way you do," Nancy said. "I just can't think of the Alien Girl as a being that is capable of being sentient at all. She's just a complex system of code. I mean no disrespect, but–"

"You're allowed to question me," Veronica interrupted flatly. "I'm not *him.*"

Nancy paused and fiddled with the buttons on her shirt. The waiter came and refilled their drinks silently. It seemed that not even *he* wanted to break the tense quiet between them.

"You don't like him very much, do you?"

Veronica was taken aback. "Don't *like* him?"

"Am I here because you want to rehire me out of the goodness of your heart, or are you just trying to prove something?" Though Veronica scanned Nancy's words for a negative underlying motive, she could not find one. Her tone was genuine. Regardless, she proceeded with caution.

"Did any of us like him?" Veronica replied. "I don't know what *you* believe about me, but I'm tired of being treated like I was the one who made him disappear just because we didn't see eye-to-eye."

"I don't think it was you," Nancy said. "I think it was the Alien Girl."

Veronica nearly choked on her water, but she continued to play it cool. "What makes you think that?" She removed any trace of excitement from her voice with near-surgical caution.

"I know it's just a crazy conspiracy theory," Nancy said, "But...you're right. None of us really liked him. He just didn't know how to be a good or reasonable person, I think. It goes against every law of robotics, and it might not make sense, but neither does his disappearance. Did you notice that the robot was the *only* thing that he kept close to him? And I'm sure it only got worse after I was fired, didn't it?"

Veronica nodded.

"Well, that proves my point further, then." She stared into her cup and used her straw to swirl her water, absent-mindedly making little whirlpools. "He treated that thing like it was alive. He forgot about the line between simulation and real life. Maybe it was an accident, maybe it wasn't, maybe he went so crazy that he forgot it was a robot and its mechanics killed him, some-how...or maybe he turned against it and it killed him to protect itself. I wouldn't be surprised if he had no system to override it with, considering that he was shooting for complete realism." She sighed. "Or maybe he just went nuts and ran away with it somewhere. Maybe he was paranoid...No, not *maybe*. He just *was*." she paused, gaining a self-conscious air. "I'm not someone that easily trusts technology. Maybe it's making me biased."

Veronica gave her a grim smile. Nancy was a lot more insight-ful than she thought. "I don't trust technology either," she said after a moment, "but I trust what people *do* with technology even less." She took a long sip of her drink. "So, when can you start?"

—

It was dark when Veronica got home. Since she'd taken her lunch break out with Nancy, she had a lot to catch up on when she got back to work. Regardless of her position, it still made her feel guilty to take advantage of her lunch breaks for anything other than catching up on work. Her back hurt. *I really need a standing desk,* she thought as she fed Bratty her dinner.

As she reset her security system, she caught a glance of Alien Girl's chip out of the corner of her eye. Her mind went back to the conversation she'd had with Nancy earlier.

You don't like him very much, do you?

The corner of her mouth twitched. *Nope,* she thought to herself. *But is it really that obvious?*

Was she wrong to judge Alien Girl just because she was created by the billionaire? During her conversation with Nancy, she agreed with nearly everything she said except one thing: that the Alien Girl couldn't possibly be sentient.

Sure, she's just code, she thought, *but we're just flesh and bone and blood and brain. We're all just atoms.*

She got flashbacks to when she sawed open Eclipta's skull. She shuddered.

She stood in the middle of her dark living room, her shoulders slumped over. Her eyes bore into the chip that she extracted by hand.

Decidedly, she placed the chip inside of her travel bag, walked to her bedroom, and fell asleep in her work clothes with no hesitation.

5

SILICON

The next morning when she went to work, she almost felt as if she had some kind of contraband on her. She considered the fact that the very thing that would undoubtedly prove her innocence was literally right in her back pocket. Despite that, she knew, there was no way anyone would ever believe her; if anything, she would only be incriminated further by posing such an insane scenario as the one that led up to the billionaire's death.

Either way, she knew that she would be used as a scapegoat. The government would want to keep that kind of technology secret. They'd use the chip for themselves and throw Veronica out. She already lived in fear as the government became more and more debased, more and more willing to frame her for something she did not do. She knew that keeping quiet, complying with them, and continuing to run the company without going against the grain was her best bet. She was already pushing it with her "progressive" ideas, like increasing her workers' pay as soon as she stepped in as CEO (after all, she saw no *need* to pad her check with more than she could possibly comprehend, let alone spend). But so long as she appeared capitalistic and liberal at most, never veering too far left, she thought that she would be okay. She'd justified the pay raise as a "necessary business decision for employee retention, ultimately cutting the costs associated with a higher turnover rate and improving morale." She was still proud of how she got her way around *that* one. Neither the Republic of California nor the United States looked kindly to working with, or tolerating the existence of, a company "gone socialist." Particularly not one with as much influence or income as Axis.

She already had to protect herself from all of the possible ways she could be targeted. She would be playing right into their hand if she ever revealed that Alien Girl was more than she seemed. Just a simple raid of her apartment, murder made to look like suicide, a fake note, and a post-mortem DSM-6 diagnosis, and she'd be out of sight, out of mind— all a low price to get their hands on some secret shiny technology for the Department of Defense. They wouldn't even need to *try* to get the public to buy their story.

"Got a lot on your mind?" Veronica jumped. She was so deep in thought that she'd forgotten to greet Josiah when he picked her up.

"Guess you could say that," she mumbled.

"What, did you get caught thinking about something embarrassing? Which is it? The new hire, or those girls from your JRPGs?"

"Don't be gross," she responded with exasperation.

"It's human, Veronica," he said.

"Then I guess I'm an alien." Her tone dripped with sarcasm.

—

Veronica had long forbidden herself from ever entering the wing that housed the Alien Girl. It was for two reasons: to prevent aggravating her obsession with her predecessor, and to quell her compulsion to investigate areas that would either make her look suspicious or would, again, loop back into her obsession. She broke the rule that she set for herself that day.

It was abandoned. The door that led to that part of HQ was perpetually locked, and she had a feeling that her employees weren't especially keen on exploring it, either. It felt cursed. Like *he* still stalked those halls, his fake girlfriend hanging off his arm. Veronica often felt indifferent when she explored places that others would superstitiously consider *cursed*, but she still felt chills trickle down her spine as she unlocked the door and stepped inside. If anyone happened to confront her later, she would tell them she needed to retrieve some supplies from the area for inventory. Not exactly a lie. She just wouldn't elaborate that it was for personal use. For digital necromancy.

The cold hit her first, then the musty still-air scent that was marinating inside for so long. The dust ruined the perfect marble-smooth white finish of everything around her. So white, it glowed even in the area's orange-purple frail darkness, the vast dirt-tinted windows only allowing a little light to filter through. The company had a very boring vision of the future when he was the one running it, Veronica realized. Everything was soulless. It matched his ruthless and bleak aspirations.

As she made her way down the hall, she remembered what everything looked like when that area was very first built. How it smelled like ammonia and the gentle breath of machines, always humming to themselves just below the sound of mechanical typing and her team's low conversations. Given that her entire job was to optimize those devices as much as possible, that sound was a reminder of how much she and her team sought to quiet that hum, cool down the warmth they emitted, make the space they took up smaller.

But she missed all of that. The warmth of an overheating machine, just like warm flesh. Their hums weren't annoying. They were endearing, even. *When I'm nervous,* she thought, *I sing to myself too.* But according to market research, the greater public didn't agree with those sentiments– and that was their target audience.

Either way, the eerie silence didn't sit right.

She found the room she was looking for. It was the billionaire's personal stash of devices, many of which were prototypes. She took the chip out of her pocket and carefully removed it from the protective case she'd placed it in. She squinted at the silicon in its translucent casing. *From sand you came,* she thought, *and to sand you returned.* She'd never observed the chip this closely before. She remembered this model, alright. It was her own team's idea that led to its development. A professor at UCLA made a ground-breaking discovery in 2039. He invented a machine that could alter the half-life of an element significantly. It was science that nobody had ever imagined before. It was his life's work. He'd found a way to make any element functionally stable, preventing radioactive decay altogether. That was something that was previously understood to be impossible, against all laws of physics. He pitched it as a way to put radiation sickness to an end forever, drastically improve sustainability, and change the very foundation of world economics– especially in regards to medication half-life, which he focused most of his attention on. He had big ideas. He wanted to save the world.

But the developers of the B132 took its potential in the opposite direction. Nobody heard anything from the machine's original creator in years. Veronica shuddered.

As far as everyone else at the company knew, the billionaire didn't get very far with this particular line of experiments. They worked on it tirelessly. It opened up an entirely new world of materials for them to tinker with as they developed new devices, but none of them were practical for home use. She and her team knew that from the beginning and tried to tell the billionaire as much, but expenses were not an issue to him. Sure, maybe they should have found it a little bit odd that he was so insistent on throwing so much money at a project that could not feasibly be used the way he was hoping (commercially, as a private device enjoyed by everyday suburbanites), but that was only one of many money-sinks throughout his career. It was new and excit-ing technology, so of course he thought it was inherently profit-able. He wasn't a scientist. At the end of the day, his intelligence was only worth as much as his last name.

The entire periodic table could be used at their whim, open-ing up an entire world when it came to inventing new methods of power supply, processing power, and more. She couldn't say that it wasn't an interesting endeavor. If only she knew that she and her team were just producing fodder for the billionaire's future obsessions. A sick feeling trickled into the back of her throat. Veronica wondered if he'd always planned to have an artificial girlfriend at the end of it all. Maybe he didn't *just* want the prestige of being the first to create super-realistic digital life. He could've gained that same prestige through countless other methods. Maybe he really was that lonely, desperate, and stubborn. Did he plan to murder Eclipta and use her body from the very beginning? She couldn't believe she was involved in something so depraved.

Her involvement made it easy to find the computer that went with the chip, at least. Not that it would have been hard to find either way. The thing took up its own room. When she pressed her thumbs against the security sensor and scanned her retinas, the door to the computer slid open. Veronica had a rare moment of appreciation for being the new top dog at Axis. She could access anything that she wanted without even having to find a way to crack it. Somehow, he'd found a way to transfer security system access to his next-in-line in case he ever had to step down as CEO. He was lucky no bad actors found a way to hack it. Or perhaps someone else with a stronger grip on cybersecurity set it up for him?

She rubbed her eyes with displeasure, then noticed all of the blinking lights spread across every unit in the room. She thought that they looked like skyscrapers at first, then decided that it all looked more like a dark sky full of multi-colored stars. Behind the computer system that took up the first half of the room was a projector positioned against the back wall. She turned it on. The surface in front of her glowed blue with reflected light. Various controllers were tucked into shelves on her right-hand side.

There was a keyboard, what looked like an XBox controller, and a suit with a virtual reality headset. *I've got options,* she thought. For then, she chose the keyboard.

Her chest swelled with pride as she looked around one last time before she booted up the system. Her team had done this. Thousands of processors, thousands of hours of labor, all to create the most top-of-the-line supercomputer in the world. If only it was used for something more practical, more helpful, than whatever the billionaire decided was best. *Maybe we can revisit this tech,* she thought. She had to wonder if her predecessor ever really wanted to develop it for public use, after all, or if he'd planned to have her team work so hard only to keep it to himself all along.

She held her breath and inserted the chip into the correct slot. The wall in front of her turned dark. Just as she began to wonder if something went wrong, white text appeared against the backdrop.

"1%", it read. Ominous.

"Oh, this is going to be the most agonizing wait of my *life,*" she groaned. Then she remembered the thumbdrive full of the billionaire's files, readily available.

Would revisiting them only upset her?

Not any more than launching Alien Girl's chip will, she thought.

She decided to look through them again as she waited.

The first time she looked through all of the folders, she'd deduced that Project Metaworld was the one most closely associated with Alien Girl, so she chose to explore that first. As she revisited the diary entries and read through them with more scrutiny, she learned that Daisy really was the Alien Girl's name, after all. She learned more about who she was as a person. However, as she scrolled deeper into the diary entries, she began to feel perverted and voyeuristic. She was peeping in on someone's secrets. Veronica had no issue with learning everything there was to know about the billionaire, but Daisy felt different. Veronica was better at differentiating what was digital and what was reality than most, but it didn't feel like Daisy was a machine. It was as if she was an innocent person pulled into something she didn't ask to be a part of.

It made her stomach do flips, so she stopped herself just as quickly as she started.

And she waited.

After it was stuck at 99% for what felt like forever, a new window opened. It still stuck to the same plain color scheme as before, a white-bordered box against endless black.

"OPTIONS:

MAKE YOURSELF KNOWN?"

She was taken back. The text cursor blinked expectantly next to the end of the sentence as if that question was in any way self-explanatory. She clacked the "N" key and pressed enter.

"SOME ELEMENTS ARE MISSING FROM THIS PROJECT. RUN ANYWAY?"

She squinted.

"Y"

A shape slowly began to load into her vision. It was the outline of a soft-curved human body, fading into existence directly across from her, parallel to her, seeming like a reflection of herself at first. Bone loaded, then muscle tightly wound itself around the skeleton like decorative ribbon. Then rippled patterns of orange fat, then olive skin. A pair of eyes rolled into place and bore through Veronica. It no longer looked anything like a reflection. It was a real woman, indistinguishable from any other human being, looking as if she were only separated from Veronica in the fact that she existed as a projected representation of what was inside the computer. She was shorter than Veronica and chubby. Black, straight hair framed her round face. She looked nothing like Eclipta.

Her lips started moving. There was no audio. "Hello?" they asked silently.

Veronica stared in horror as a sense of panic washed over the woman's expression. She kept repeating herself, becoming desperate, her face contorting itself more and more. Veronica instinctively put her hands up and stepped backwards, never taking her eyes off the wall. She started to look like she was screaming wordlessly, her face turning red, tears streaming down her cheeks. Right before she forcefully made the program stop running, she saw the woman mouth one last thing. Veronica was not skilled at lip-reading, but what she was saying was clear as day.

"There has to be more than this. I can't be dead."

—

The chip's warmth slowly faded as it sat in the palm of her hand. It was unnerving, as if it were a recently deceased cadaver still in the process of cooling. She shoved it back in her pocket. That sense of unease lingered for the rest of the day.

Straight-backed, she sat at her desk with her hands folded, twiddling her thumbs. Too much shock flooded her system for her to even begin considering what went wrong. The woman she saw must have been Daisy. The *real* Daisy. Veronica never even considered the fact that Daisy's original, true form would look so different from the body the billionaire provided her. For "machine learning purposes", the billionaire had once instructed everyone at the company to treat Daisy just like she's one of them. He said that it could damage her development if they told her that she isn't from another universe and that she's actually artificial. *We want her to be fully immersed in the idea that she truly is a flesh-and-blood being,* he'd said. *Our goal is to see what happens if we convince a machine that it is real, but alien to our universe. Can we make something real by choosing to believe that it's real?*

He was very explicit that anyone who dared to "jeopardize his project" would be promptly fired. Nobody had the balls to do it, as unnerving as it could be to lie to the Alien Girl about her very existence. Save for Nancy.

Nancy's reason for termination must not have been provided because the billionaire didn't want anyone to start putting too many pieces together. Nobody was meant to see the sheer human-like panic it caused Daisy to feel when her humanity was questioned. Perhaps the billionaire, as myopic as he was, failed to realize how intensely Daisy would react to an existential crisis—which was all too realistically. That was no "glitch." It was no misunderstanding. She wasn't confused in the same way a robot may be confused if you provide it with information it is not programmed to understand. That was sheer confusion, sadness, and fear. The way any human would react to being told they're not real.

Project Metaworld was real to Daisy. That was her home.

When that thought crossed her mind, something clicked. The reason why Daisy loaded into a void was because there was no Project Metaworld to load with her. Did that mean that Daisy retained memories from her previous life? How else would she know that her environment wasn't normal?

Back when the billionaire was still alive, Veronica thought that Metaworld was just a relatively advanced self-building sandbox project. Clearly, it was way more than that. Not like Veronica ever got to see the full thing in action. That was reserved for the billionaire's eyes only. *Privacy issues,* or something like that.

All of the residents of Metaworld must have been just as complex as Daisy.

She looked out her window. It was starting to get dark outside. Save for a few overachieving stragglers strolling toward the parking garage, almost everyone else had gone home, already.

She rose from her chair, her body quivering, and shoved the chip back into her back pocket. She took the drive she'd saved all of the billionaire's files onto and gripped it in her palm, her low heels clicking against the marble ground.

When she arrived back at the room she'd visited earlier, the once majestic-looking area now looked a bit sinister. The units, which she's previously found reminiscent of a comforting night sky, towered over her threateningly. There was so much more power inside that room than she could have ever imagined, and her team was the one that created that power. She couldn't believe that the billionaire managed to keep the terrifying potential of the very technology she was making under such tight wraps.

She attached the drive to the supercomputer, then inserted Daisy's chip.

Another textbox.

"DUPLICATE HUMAN FOUND. OVERWRITE MEMORIES?"

Project Metaworld ended just as Daisy was pulled out of it. It dawned on Veronica that this version of the project files must have contained an iteration of Daisy that had no memories of the billionaire, who was blissfully unaware of the fact that her world wasn't real whatsoever. A happier version of Daisy, maybe. One without existential dread and less baggage.

Acid guilt burned through her stomach when she tracked down Daisy's old files and copied them to her drive. Hesitantly, she pressed the enter key.

"Y"

She needed the version of Daisy that knew who the billionaire was. She needed more information. Unfortunately, Daisy would just have to carry the burden of that knowledge. And above all, there was just no right answer to the trolley problem-like dilemma in front of her.

A new loading screen popped up. Veronica gathered her

things and left the room, triple-checking that it was locked behind her.

And a few hours later, after Veronica finally managed to fall into a restless slumber with bratty cuddled close, Daisy woke up.

6

CONFESSIONAL

Daisy's eyes popped open, and she screamed and flailed wildly off of the couch she'd been sleeping on. She landed on her back. Her eyes fixed themselves on the off-white ceiling above her, her chest rising and falling rapidly. She clutched her stomach and her ears roared with rushing blood. *Dream?* she thought, her conscious brain still somewhat absent.

A mourning dove's call swam through the thick bright air outside of the apartment's window. Sunlight trickled in through the glass panes, illuminating all of the soft edges of the living room's interior. Last night's uneaten dinner still dominated the room's aroma. Deep and rich caramelized onions and tomato sauce still lingered. All of the furniture in the living room crowded her body, almost feeling as if it was cradling her, doting on her– all sweet earthy shades of gold and brown. Soft, muted rainbow crochet hung off of every single thing in sight. Daisy recognized the small and simple faces of the porcelain figures her grandmother liked to collect. The sound of appliances humming, faucets dripping, fans whirring, and quiet canned laughter from a sitcom playing in her grandmother's bedroom all harmonized with one another and created a beautiful and comforting chord. Above all, everything was so very warm. She was home.

"Just a dream," she said out loud to herself. Tears dripped off of her cheeks and onto the dusty hardwood beneath her. Her grandmother's slow, shuffling walk echoed through the hallway with joint-clicking rhythm.

"Daisy?" her grandmother called, voice tinged with concern. She was used to Daisy having night terrors, but she hadn't had one that intense in quite a while.

She pressed her palms to the floor and forced herself up. She had a throbbing headache. Her whole body felt sore. Choked sobs bubbled up out of her throat like an infant's spit-up. Her back collapsed back into the couch as her vision blurred with tears. As quickly as an old woman is able, her grandmother sat down next to her and placed her hand on Daisy's back. She rubbed her thumb between Daisy's shoulder blades. "What wrong?" she asked.

"Just a nightmare," Daisy responded, but her shrill, whiny voice and choked sobs gave her away.

"Not 'just' a nightmare," her grandmother replied. "In, out, deep breaths."

She followed her instructions. In a few minutes' time, she calmed down.

"I...think I need an emergency therapy session."

She blinked in pleasant surprise. "You *want* therapy?"

Daisy looked down at the ground and used her big toe to trace shapes into the old, unswept floor. "Yeah. It was bad."

Before she even finished her sentence, her grandmother was already starting toward the phone.

—

It felt unreal to Daisy that she was in a therapist's office *already*. She wasn't sure what her grandmother had done to get an appointment so soon, but the events leading up to her sitting on that couch happened so fast that it left her head spinning. *Was it even that serious? Am I really being this dramatic about a dream?*

Her grandmother reheated some of the dinner Daisy had missed out on right after she got off the phone, fed it to her for lunch, called a taxi, and sent her on her way. And here she was, in a therapist's office for the first time since she was a small child. At last.

The sound of her therapist's pen clicking brought her back to reality. "How did I get here so fast?" she blurted out.

The therapist, a spindly bespectacled old woman, smiled at her. "Are you asking how I was able to have an appointment with you so soon?" Her voice was strong and steady for such a frail looking woman.

"I made time. Did you know that your grandmother's a friend of mine?" She began writing on her notepad. "I was able to squeeze you in."

Guilt collected at the bottom of Daisy's gut. *Really. I must be acting dramatic to put everyone to all this trouble.*

"So, Daisy," she continued, "what brings you in today?"

The guilt made her stomach acid curdle. Her face turned hot. She was embarrassed over how trivial her reason for being there really seemed to be when she said it out loud. "I had a nightmare," she muttered, expecting a judgmental look from the therapist.

But the look never came. Her expression stayed as warm as ever. "A nightmare," she repeated. "Okay. Have you been to therapy before?"

"Yeah," she replied. "A long time ago. When I was a little kid. I kind of...*had* to go. This is the first time I've gone by choice."

"Congratulations. It's a really big step to make that kind of choice. Now, Daisy, I have a feeling that you're not here because of the nightmare alone. Please correct me if I'm wrong, but the nightmare was more of a...trigger to come to therapy, yeah?"

"I guess so."

The therapist leaned back in her chair and crossed her legs. "Okay. Either way, let's start from there. Let me just ask you a preliminary question first: Are you at risk of hurting yourself or anyone else?"

Daisy blushed. "No, not right now," she said. As soon as the words exited her lips, she felt like kicking herself. *Not "right now"? Are you fucking stupid?*

The therapist didn't seem to mind. "Alrighty, then, with that out of the way...what was your nightmare about?"

"Well," Daisy began to stammer. "It's kind of embarrassing to say out loud. Give me a second."

"Sure," she replied.

Daisy twiddled with her thumbs for a while, staring down at the floor. After she collected herself, the words started to spill out of her mouth like a broken dam.

"I dreamt that...this world was fake. The stars were fake, the sky was just a ceiling. Everything. There's this..." she paused, decided not to continue her thought, and restarted. "There was a voice in my head in the dream that told me to walk through town to the top of a cliff. And to jump off of it. Well, when I jumped off, I started floating, all the way up until I touched the sky's ceiling, then I was transported to a different world. And there was a billionaire living there. He told me he was in love with me, and he made me be his girlfriend...and everyone treated me like I wasn't real. And he was. Well, mean to me." Tears welled up in her eyes again. "Not just mean to me. Abusive. He controlled everything I did. Then I learned that everyone was treating me like I wasn't real because I really *wasn't*. The whole time, I was really just artificial intelligence, and my whole life was a simulation– I learned that by looking through the billion-aire's stuff. He tried to kill me, so I killed him instead. Out of self-defense. Then I killed myself." Her voice became shrill. She always hated when she cried, because it made her voice sound annoying and pleading, overly emotional. "And when I killed myself, I woke up to learn that *there is nothing after death*. I was just in a void...there was no darkness, no light, no nothing. I can't describe it. Nothing."

They sat in silence for a few beats. "Wow," the therapist replied. "I can tell that it took a lot of courage to share that with me."

Daisy felt awkward. She said nothing.

"So," the therapist continued, "I'm going to ask you a few questions, okay? Daisy, have you been in a relationship in the past? Are you in a relationship right now?"

"Yeah, I've dated before," she said. "But I don't date anymore."

"You say that like it's by choice. Is it?"

"Kind of," Daisy said. "It's not that I don't *want* to, but I choose not to date. It hasn't turned out well for me."

"Okay. I want to loop back to something you shared with me earlier. Remember that you only have to share what you're comfortable sharing. You said that you're not at risk of hurting anyone *right now*. Have you been at risk in the past?"

Fuck. I should've known that wasn't the right answer. She decided to be honest, anyway. "Yes," she said. "Of hurting myself. I think that's why the nightmare was so triggering."

"And when was the last time you've seriously thought about hurting yourself?"

"Oh, I don't know," Daisy said. "Months." Quickly, she added, "a long time, so to speak." *Like that'll stop her from putting you in a psych ward.*

"Daisy, I can tell that you're anxious," the therapist said. "Let me reiterate that this is a safe place to share your thoughts and feelings. You don't have anything to worry about."

Shit! Stop being anxious. Look less anxious!

"Okay," Daisy whispered. "Thank you."

It was quiet between them for a moment.

"So what do you think the dream means?" Daisy finally said.

"Well," the therapist began, "I don't want to assume anything about your life, so keep in mind that this is just what I'm guessing. But from the looks of it, you're experiencing some pretty intense anxiety. Maybe you're just anxious about death in general, anxious about relationships because of bad past experiences. Maybe you're experiencing some derealization. Many people do at some point in their lives, by the way." She leaned toward Daisy and met her gaze.

"I can tell that this dream really upset you. I find that when we try to pathologize things like nightmares, it can actually be counterproductive. I don't think that you're strange, or crazy, or that you have anything to be embarrassed about, honey. I don't think that you should think of yourself that way, either." She smiled. "It was a bad dream, and it upset you so deeply that you felt a need to visit me today. So let's focus on healing from that, not on psychoanalyzing ourselves. Okay?"

"Okay," Daisy replied.

The therapist's words only reaffirmed that Daisy would never bring up the voice in her head to anyone.

Come to think of it, Daisy thought later as she made her way out of the office, *where has it gone?*

7

ANGEL

Peace flooded Veronica's system when she woke up, then resentment. She wanted to hang onto that post-slumber bliss for longer, but it faded all too soon as stress hormone brute-forced its way back into her system. It almost would have been better if she could have just woken up stressed in the first place. She'd prefer that over feeling the pain that comes with remembering how much she had to do, how much she had to account for, knowing that she has to constantly watch her back, all piece-by-piece. Like her memories were loading one at a time, each one packing its own special punch.

Bratty sat on Veronica's chest. She meowed in between a constant stream of deep purrs. "Fishy breath," Veronica muttered with affection and displeasure. All at once, she sat up straight, which caused her cat to scatter with an indignant mew.

She rubbed her eyes so hard she started seeing shapes. One last memory wormed its way back into her waking mind.

Daisy.

An anxious pit formed at the bottom of her stomach. The anxiety, however, was not over whether or not someone would stumble across the room and witness Daisy's reborn form before she could. She was confident that nobody would be able to get past the security system. No– her anxiety was in response to the idea that there could be another malfunction, that something else could have gone horribly wrong, leaving Daisy stranded in an unlivable world for hours, possibly breaking her psyche. Why hadn't she thought of that last night?

Why do I even care?

Daisy's display of pure fear, her body floating in that void...

...It was just so *disturbing.*

Her carelessness with the Alien Girl resulted in Veronica's failure to process the consequences of her actions. Never had she dealt with technology anything like that before. She knew that she could not make that same mistake again.

She got dressed and waited for Josiah to pick her up. It had always been so easy for her to tell the difference between what was real and what was not. She had a naturally fine-tuned intuition when it came to what was produced by technology versus what was authentic. She'd never, ever been wrong before, and she'd never second-guessed herself, either. As it became more and more difficult to tell what was artificial and what wasn't, as world governments became more skilled at tricking their own citizens into believing false narratives they'd spin using computer-generated videos, pictures, audio recordings, what have you, as scammers and ne'er-do-wells and even trusted confidants all used technology for seedy reasons, she was sure to always look at tech with a keen eye and complete scrutiny.

It was the first time in her life that she was faced with a product of engineering that she not only didn't understand, but stumped her into a screeching halt.

And, further still, one that she truly believed was sentient and as authentic as any other flesh-and-blood human regardless.

She fiddled with her cross pendant in the back of Josiah's car and gazed out the window. For once, she couldn't wait to get to work.

—

"OPTIONS:
MAKE YOURSELF KNOWN?"
"…
N"

A new screen flashed. It was entirely different from the pure blackness Veronica saw the last time she'd booted it up.

"WELCOME TO METAWORLD

ANCHOR PERSPECTIVE:

1. *SEARCH SENTIENT ITEMS BY TYPE +
ID*
2. *RECENTS*"

"Perspective?" Veronica mumbled to herself. When she glanced at the list under the "recents" category, there was only one option.

"'DAISY BELL' (HUMAN #119.126.487.616)"

Her.

The meaning of "anchor perspective" clicked. She highlighted Daisy's name, deliberated for a few seconds, then finally selected it.

She saw what must have been the back of Daisy's head. It was like playing a video game in third-person perspective. More interestingly, there was a rapid stream of data materializing in the top left corner of the screen. One line read, "AUTO-TRANSLATION ENABLED." One kept track of every human's death and birth. There was an option to keep track of other species, as well, but she left it off. It would probably flicker so fast, there would be no way to keep track of anything. Unless she unchecked the "real-time" option, she realized– she did so, and a meter popped onto her screen. It allowed her to speed up or slow down her perception of the world's time as she pleased. She decided to keep it as is.

"Creepy," Veronica whispered to herself.

There was a "Settings/More Options" button as well. When she clicked it, an endless amount of buttons and widgets overwhelmed her line of sight. Pure power all at her disposal. *If there's a God, is this what He sees when He looks down at our world?*

Does He get overwhelmed by it, too?

Her attention focused back on Daisy. She was laying on her

stomach on a brown sofa. She was just...sleeping, it looked like. It felt weird, watching someone sleep. She almost felt ashamed. What was she doing? Just existing as a ghost, creepily stalking the people living in this little world? Why did she keep "making herself unknown", as the program referred to it? Cowardice?

The reason she was examining the program, she reminded herself, was to learn more about the billionaire. About how he died and what he left behind. More about his creation– the Alien Girl, specifically. And in order to learn more, she'd have to communicate with Daisy, and to communicate with Daisy, she'd have to...well, get the fuck over herself and communicate with Daisy.

She didn't even have a real plan when she decided to return to the room. She was merely following impulse like a child with a new toy. She felt silly. This wasn't a video game she could pick up and meander around in as she pleased. It was alive, self-aware, the first ever instance of artificial beings existing through artificial means. Something so independent that it was able to exterminate its creator for its own survival.

And it was sleeping so soundly.

Perhaps cowardice was not the only reason she'd refused to present herself to Daisy so far. Maybe Veronica was afraid to scare her. *Yeah*, she thought, *that's it*. It was absurd. How could she possibly be afraid of frightening a piece of technology? Still, how would *she* react if a god-like being descended from the heavens to ask her about murder? Or was it presumptuous to assume that Daisy would see her as god-like, at all?

How is she dealing with what happened?

She focused on Daisy again. Watched her back slowly rise

and fall. Had she told anyone about what happened to her? Did she even realize that what happened to her was real? Did she even remember it? Could a being like her even repress memories at all?

How does one even cope with something like that?

She opened the "Options" menu again and squinted at the myriad ways she could alter Metaworld. One button caught her eye.

"ENABLE DREAM VISITATION IN CREATURES WITH ANCHORED PERSPECTIVE"

I can appear to her in her dreams? Veronica bit her thumb, deep in thought. *Maybe that would be a better idea. Dreams are the one place where the absurd isn't too out of place.*

She toggled it on.

Another dialogue box.

"MAKE YOURSELF KNOWN?"

She placed her nose between her hands and clutched the bottom half of her face. She deliberated for a little while, pacing back and forth in the cool, dark room, almost as if she were in a trance. Her eyes flickered to the VR suit in the corner of the room.

I wonder what it's like to be fully immersed.

Without a second thought, she stepped into it and zipped it up. It automatically connected. She was disoriented at first, but quickly adjusted. It felt just like she was living in Daisy's world.

All of her senses were perfectly synced to her new environment. She could feel the sunshine filtering through Daisy's window on her skin, sense the vintage odor of crochet, wood, and savory food, look around her with complete ease...

...Incredible. It felt entirely different from just watching through a screen.

Daisy turned over on the couch. She studied her face for a few seconds, amazed by just how real she looked. Then she cracked a smirk.

With dark circles like those, I better hope she sleeps often enough for me to see her again.

"N"

The screen flashed black.

Veronica remembered something as she was woven into Daisy's brain, her very existence hidden in its seams. It's impossible for somebody to remember the exact moment they fall asleep. Yet she recognized the way she fell into Daisy's mind—it was what it feels like to begin a dream. And when the dream finally appeared before her, she struggled to remember what it felt like to get there in the first place. Just as if it were her own.

She was in a dark room that she didn't recognize. It looked like a shoddy little apartment. She never really believed in such things as good or bad vibrations, but there was a negative aura to the area that made all of the hairs on her body stand up straight. All of the walls were painted with an uninviting sickly yellow-white color and they were peppered with fist-sized holes. The carpet was threadbare, an ugly dull blue. The distinct sound of a box fan broke the still air. It was coming from a different room.

It smelled like processed food and dirty laundry. It smelled like dust. It smelled like sickness, and it felt *horrid*. Veronica's throat tightened until she felt like she was choking. She was lightheaded and sick with anxiety. *Is this a nightmare? Is Daisy's fear infectious?*

There was a couch in the middle of the room. Somehow, that couch felt more...*perverted* than the one she saw the Alien Girl sleeping on earlier. It was misshapen and broken, bent downward in the middle. As if it were carrying the weight of all of the illness festering inside of that place. But just like the couch she'd seen earlier, Daisy was sleeping on this one, too. She had countless electrodes stuck to her body, some over her chest, some hidden beneath a sweat-soaked shirt. They all connected to a machine. It was ever so slightly different– bigger, maybe?-- but Veronica still recognized it as the one she saw in the billionaire's hide-out. The one that was supposedly meant to charge Daisy, according to what he told Veronica's team. Maybe it was made to discourage her from getting up and wandering around in the middle of the night.

Or maybe it was just made to fulfill the billionaire's sick desires.

Veronica tip-toed over to where Daisy was restlessly tossing about. Her line of vision bobbed in time with her footsteps. It made her feel a little motion sick. She was hyper-aware of every little noise she made. Her vision swam around her. She heard her own breath grow heavier. She knew there was no way that Daisy could see her, but she still had an intense fear of being caught.

As if on cue, Daisy's eyes snapped open. They bore right through Veronica. She screamed, tugging at the electrodes with sweat-misted desperation, but they would not tear away– like they were superglued to her skin. Like they were a part of her body. The environment shifted between Daisy's dream and the waking world, where she was sleeping in the apartment. A strange sensation exploded through Veronica's nervous system. A new message popped into the corner of her vision just above the endless data stream.

"ERROR," it read. "CODE 475: SLEEP PARALYSIS."

In the waking world, Daisy was sweating bullets. Her eyes were wide and glossed over with tears. Her lips were blood-red and chapped. Her mouth lay agape, but only a low, hoarse, whispered moan managed to exit it.

In the dream world, a shadowy figure exited the bedroom and floated into the living area. It was shaped like a man.

Veronica looked over at the figure, then back at Daisy. "It's okay," she whispered.

Daisy did not hear her. She continued to panic.

"It's okay," she said, more loudly, this time.

Fuck. Fuck. Fuck. I'm about to do something stupid.

SETTINGS/MORE OPTIONS > MAKE SELF KNOWN > AD-VANCED > MAKE SELF KNOWN DURING DREAM VISITATION ONLY

...

ARE YOU SURE?

...

Y

Veronica squatted next to the couch.

"Daisy, you're just dreaming. It's going to be okay. You need to wake up now."

Daisy's eyes, only staring through Veronica before that point, finally fixed themselves onto her. "Are you an angel?" Daisy breathed.

Then she woke up.

—

"This morning, the president of the Republic of California proposed the 'Affordable Emergency Act', which would aid lower-income citizens in applying for insurance for police service, protection, and assistance. This act would also require insurers to disregard factors such as economic stability, race, and area of residence. Such an act passing could set a precedent for the United States to make some changes, as well. Now here's the controversy– the funds for such an act would be produced through taxation. Tonight, experts will weigh in on…"

As the radio droned on, Veronica stared out the window. She didn't have the energy to ask Josiah to turn it off. She couldn't do anything but feel indifferent to the world around her.

"I didn't see you all day," Josiah said as he pulled into the parking lot of her apartment complex. "I think you could stand to take a few breaks every once in a while. You know? I worry about you. You've been so hard at work, Veronica."

"Eh," she muttered. "I'll be fine."

Not hard at work, she thought. *Hard at escapism.*

8

AILMENT

I can't even just take a fucking nap? Daisy peeled off her sweat-soaked shirt. She was standing in front of her bathroom mirror, listening to the muffled sound of her bath running. She stared into her own face, peppered with the beginnings of a stress-induced breakout, contorted in fear and annoyance. *I can't even avoid my trauma in my dreams? I did the right thing. I went to therapy. I'm supposed to be doing better. Is it too late for that?*

She sighed. *One therapy session isn't going to cure you, dummy. You should know that better than anyone.*

She'd just woken up a few minutes ago. She was still recollecting everything that happened in her dream while trying to find a way to relax at the same time. It'd been a long time since she had a sleep paralysis episode like that. Possibly it would take all day to regroup. She took deep breaths and rubbed her face. Reminded herself of her own physicality. "Okay," she whispered.

It was deeply disconcerting that her nightmare from the night before continued during her nap. Was she having nightmares about her own nightmares? Was that even possible?

Since when can your nightmares be split up into a fucking series?

She furrowed her brow at the idea. That wasn't something that happened to other people, right?

Let's focus on healing, not on psychoanalyzing ourselves.

Daisy's chest filled with shame. It was like her lungs were replaced with two gallons of water. *She doesn't even know the half of it. She thinks I'm a typical person. A person who doesn't hear weird voices.*

She stepped into her bath and remembered the mysterious woman who appeared at the end of her dream.

Her grandmother told her once that every single person someone sees in their dreams is somebody they've seen in real life, before. Even if you only saw them for a split second. *Mind can't make up faces,* her grandmother said. *It must recycle.*

I recognize her...vaguely.

But from what? The woman looked like she was one of the people from her nightmare. Big eyes, high cheekbones.

It clicked. That woman *was* in her nightmare. She sat next to her during the billionaire's conference. She *kidnapped her.*

She matched Veronica's concerned, pleading face from her sleep paralysis episode with the way she looked at her in the nightmare. The exact moment that it dawned on her that Daisy was not artificial at all– or, at least, she was more human than she thought. Yes, that's what she recognized her from. Her dream. It all made sense.

But your mind still can't make up faces, right?

Something told her that her grandmother's words weren't just the product of an old wives' tale. Who was the woman's real-life equivalent? She couldn't think of a single person that she'd ever known who looked anything like Veronica. Or anyone else in her nightmare, for that matter. All of them felt unique, real, so very fleshed-out. Come to think of it, the entire ordeal didn't feel like a nightmare at all. She didn't remember falling asleep.

She only remembered waking up.

Upon remembering the strange woman's identity, she felt an odd sense of longing in her chest. She hated to admit it, but she hoped to see her in her dreams again that night. The woman captivated her just as much as she did in her nightmare. Yes, she kidnapped her, but she was the only person who looked at her like a human being at all. She didn't have any real-life friends. Maybe her longing to see Veronica again stemmed from a deep-seated loneliness. She felt disgusted with herself. After all, Veronica *wasn't real.* What kind of person felt such a strong desire to be friends with someone from their nightmare? Someone who kidnapped them, then only offered them a small acknowledgement of their personhood afterward? The one interaction they had with one another– a *fake* interaction, mind you, a figment of her imagination– was negative. She couldn't believe that she was so desperate, she was drawn in by a dream girl who didn't even like her.

It was pathetic.

The bathtub was overflowing.

"Fuck," Daisy whispered, quickly turning the water off.

She felt less like a functioning adult than ever before.

—

Her grandmother was waiting for her on the couch when she finished her bath. "Therapy was good?" she asked gently. She didn't take her eyes off of the stories playing on their television. "Feel better?"

She opened her mouth, but no words came out. She wanted to tell her grandmother that she was feeling better already, that she could feel the progress that she was making, but she just didn't have the energy to lie. Instead, a deep-chested sigh exited her lips.

Her grandmother quirked an eyebrow, glancing over at Daisy. "It supposed to get bad before it is better, yes?" she said.

"I know that," Daisy said, "but it doesn't really...stop the badness, you know?"

"I understand," her grandmother replied. "Sit down. Watch a show with me. It will be okay." She paused. "You never gotta talk to me about what happen in therapy, Daisy. It can be secret."

She walked over to the sofa and placed her head on her grandmother's lap, just like she did when she was a small child. *I need to get out more,* she thought, dully closing her eyes. *Maybe I'll go clubbing sometime soon.* Whatever was on television was too boring to *not* fall asleep to, despite all the sleep she'd already gotten that day. She never knew what was going on in her grandmother's stories. Come to think of it, she guessed that her shows were a bit like Daisy's own addictive little habits. They're built to always make you want to come back for more, always have a new plot twist, a new character with amnesia, a new illegitimate child, a new romance. That's how you get people to watch a low-quality show for decades. Her grandmother was aware that the shows she watched were garbage. She'd say as much. Regardless, she still watched them. Just like how Daisy knew that cheap thrills weren't a substitute for a quality life. But the flashing colors, alcohol, greasy bar food, greasy one-night stands, they kept drawing her in, over and over and over. But they were never permanent. Just like trigger-happy writers killing off characters and derailing plotlines in a long-running soap opera, always returning to that same status quo in the end, the social interactions she had would never turn into anything more than just that. Not even one measly friendship. At the end of the day, it was her routine of clubbing, getting drunk, and stumbling back home that was truly boring and repetitive, when you observed it from the outside. The same episode over and over again.

But she wanted to experience being seventeen again. The right way, this time.

Her grandmother stroked her hair. She slipped into unconsciousness. This time, she did not dream.

—

Her head was still quiet. The voice disappeared without a trace.

She decided to go back to work the next morning, as tempting as it was to call in sick. Acting as a functioning adult would eventually make her *feel* like a functional adult, she thought. Rotting in bed was only going to make her feel worse in the long run.

The morning air was as crisp and cool as ever against Daisy's tired face as she walked back to the deli. Though she never liked the voice's presence, she still found herself missing it. Everything was too quiet, and she felt far too *alone*. Above that, though, the voice's disappearance made no sense. She could understand if she had some kind of undiagnosed mental disorder or was experiencing mild psychosis for some other reason, something like that– but one bad nightmare, and suddenly it was gone.

Almost as if the nightmare were real.

"It wasn't," Daisy mumbled to herself, irritated. "So how?"

You killed him in your nightmare. Of course he hasn't come back.

She narrowed her eyes, self-conscious of the fact that she was talking to herself under her breath in public. Regardless, she continued responding to her own thoughts out loud. "That doesn't make sense," she said.

None of this makes sense in the first place. How do you hear a voice in your head for years, ever since the exact date of your eighteenth birthday, only for it to disappear after you have the worst nightmare of your life? Just like that? It's not like it slowly went away. It's not there anymore.

She forgot what life was like before the voice made itself present. She could no longer imagine living without it. Though the sudden radio silence was disturbing, maybe it would return eventually. Maybe she was in shock.

Or maybe it's because you killed the billionaire.

"I'm not a murderer," she said a little louder than she meant. It felt odd to hear herself speaking such heavy words so calmly. All of a sudden, she was aware of her surroundings again. She was inside the deli's storage room. She blinked and turned on the lights. She lost track of time on her way there.

She rinsed off a box's worth of tomatoes, then got to work on slicing them.

"Nobody here to call me a seductress?" she said out loud. Then she laughed, a humorless and dry laugh. She stopped herself.

You're acting crazy. Stop acting crazy.

"And if I was a murderer," she continued, "I'd be totally justified."

The weight of her own words fell on her. She covered her mouth, feeling her eyes become glossier.

Just stop. Stop talking to yourself.

Tears fell onto the tomatoes, mixing with their juice. She turned around, pulled herself away from the tomato slicer, and aggressively wiped her eyes. After a few moments, she scrubbed her hands clean, forced a flat expression onto her face, and kept slicing the tomatoes.

There's not even anyone around to see you. Does it matter?

She decided that it *did* matter.

After all, she never knew if somebody was really watching or not, these days. Veronica appeared to her in her dreams. She was sure that if she could do something like that, she could also watch Daisy's life like a god the exact same way that the billionaire did. Who was to say that Veronica wasn't hovering over her shoulder right then? The billionaire may have died, but Veronica *lived*. She had the potential to become a new voice then, didn't she? If Metaworld outlived the billionaire, that meant that anyone from his universe could become a new observer. Veronica made sense. She was the most likely candidate, either way.

She was the one on the billionaire's ass, keeping track of all of his projects, watching him like a hawk, going so far as to steal the Alien Girl, collecting information from the inside...based on her authoritative demeanor, it seemed like *she* was the one spearheading whatever they were trying to accomplish by kidnapping Daisy. She probably gained access to Metaworld too. *Of course* Veronica would start watching her. Maybe Veronica was just...quieter. Maybe her methods were different.

Stop it. You're thinking crazy. It was just a goddamn dream.

All of the things that had happened to her lately were also fucking crazy. Didn't she have the right to think crazy? Or was everything that happened to her all in her head? Was she fully delusional?

I don't think I'm delusional.

The definition of delusion.

She barely made it through her work day without having a panic attack. She supposed that she acted normally enough, but it felt like her veneer was cracking, almost ready to burst. She couldn't handle doing that every single day. She still couldn't believe that she felt even *more* crazy *without* the voice there. *Shouldn't I feel normal now? I've been cured. Kind of.*

It was the unknown that scared her, she realized. She didn't understand *why* the voice went away. She didn't know if someone was still watching her. Her most logical mind assured her that nobody was, but everything else said otherwise. Her dream felt so real, it wasn't dream-like at all. It felt the same as any other memory. She didn't remember falling asleep in the first place– she had a headache all night, and any sleep she caught at all was shallow, at best. More like resting her eyes. *Unless that was part of the dream?* Usually her memory was far more reliable than that, dream or not.

There was only one way to attempt to ease her unrest, she realized.

She needed to confront it herself.

9

EXPOSED

It was routine at that point. Josiah drove Veronica to work, she pretended to do work, maybe had a beer or a few to smooth the day down better, and then she explored Metaworld.

If "exploring Metaworld" meant observing the Alien Girl, specifically.

She felt a little strange about it. Eventually she would have to see Daisy again. She couldn't keep going about it like this, stalker-like and unproductive. She had to do *something*, or she'd never learn anything else.

Or would she? Would it be better to play the long game, wait for Daisy to mention something about the billionaire to someone? Didn't her grandmother mention a therapy session at some point? Maybe she could catch Daisy while she was in therapy, speed up time a little bit–

She paused, feeling guilt trickle down her throat and collect in her stomach. Sitting in on someone's therapy session without their knowledge? Really? The idea made her feel awful. Since when did those kinds of things make her feel *awful*? She was a spy, dammit. She was no stranger to intruding on people's privacy. She supposed that it was the fact that Daisy was entirely different from anyone she'd ever known, tragic in a way she'd never seen before. She was used to spying on the elite, average people too at times, so long as it was necessary for her end goal– but Daisy finally was back to the life she belonged to, and peeking into it felt like she was interrupting the peace of a woman who had been through hardship she couldn't even begin to imagine.

Therapy was a bit much. Perhaps she could observe Daisy's dreams again, see where it goes. If Daisy just saw her as some kind of recurring character in her dreams, not someone who affects her in the waking world, then there was no harm done. *Right?*

After she finished her third beer, she decided to crawl out of her office and go back down to the long-abandoned area of the lab. Usually, she was able to do so without any interruption. This time was different.

"Hey!"

Veronica nearly jumped. She glanced beside her, attempting to salvage the professional demeanor she held before, keeping her head high and her stride purposeful. It was Nancy, who was matching her pace. She didn't seem to notice that she'd startled Veronica.

"Hello, Nancy," She replied. Most of the time, her employees were too afraid to have casual conversation with her at all– a symptom of their time working with the billionaire. Veronica wasn't sure how to feel about Nancy's forwardness. She didn't know if it came from a place of assertiveness or naivete. She was leaning toward a little bit of both.

"I really enjoyed having lunch with you," she continued. "I think we should do it again sometime. Are you going to be free anytime soon? I know that you're busy."

Lunch? Does she think that I wanted to have lunch with her for personal reasons? Like we're friends? Veronica cringed. Was that a bitchy thing to think about someone?

"I'll have to look at my schedule when I get the chance," Veronica said. "I'm hardly ever able to take lunch at all. Right now, I have some urgent business to complete."

"So you're saying that you don't take all of your employees out to lunch?" Nancy mumbled. "Did you...make time just for me?" She played with her hair and looked off to the side.

WHAT.

Veronica tried to act casual, but she was evidently flustered. "Had time that day, that's all," she said. "Please excuse me. I really need to get to what I was doing. I'll talk to you later." She amped up her powerwalk, strategically disappearing into the nearest elevator.

When she was sure that nobody could hear her, she spoke out loud to herself. "Talking to people has consequences," she whispered.

—

Once she finished zipping up her suit, she turned the projector on. Daisy was getting ready for bed. *Perfect timing,* she thought. But as Veronica watched her, waiting for her to go to bed, a gnawing sense of guilt grew in the pit of her stomach. It was weird. It was entirely predatory, regardless of how benevolent Veronica thought her own intentions were. She was watching a woman she'd never even met get ready for bed. It reminded her of a child version of herself, hiding under the dining table to change her clothes out of fear that God could see her. "Ronnie, baby," her dad said to her one day, "you've gotta stop that."

"Why?" she asked. "I don't want God to see me in my underwear."

"It's nothing God's never seen before," he said, exasperated. "You act like God's some kinda creep. You think he's a creep, Ronnie?"

No, Veronica thought to herself. *Especially not* this *God.*

She sped up her perception of Daisy's time and stopped when she was asleep in bed. As to not linger too long on the image of a peacefully sleeping woman– as to not make herself feel like a *stalker*– she entered her dream all at once. With a pang of shame, she chose to make her presence unknown once again.

Everything slowly faded in from darkness, static-ridden at first. She heard the sound of a dove cooing nearby accompanied by the crisp sound of running water. A faint breeze wisped its way across her cheeks, and her body felt perfectly warm. Just as if she were sitting in a hot bath. Her nose caught a fruity smell on the wind, and she noticed that she was surrounded by endless strawberry fields. The strawberries themselves were all white, abundant and lush. They were peppered into full bundles of blue-green vegetation. A river cut through the center of the field, and its water was light pink– beautifully translucent. A red sunset blanketed itself over an indigo sky. Far in the distance, she could see a figure crouched on its knees. Even further still, there were rows of identical white houses. But they did not look three-dimensional. When Veronica shifted her head a certain way, walked a bit to the side to observe them better, they looked like flat cardboard cut-outs. She decided to approach the human figure, who must have been Daisy.

The figure grew closer as she walked toward it, but the houses did not. She wondered if there was any way to reach the houses at all. After a small trek, she made out a pair of glasses on the ground. Daisy hunched over them and delicately tinkered with its lenses. The wire frame was bent out of shape. *But Daisy doesn't wear glasses, does she?*

Veronica leaned over to look at her face. She wore an expression that was a mix of concentration and frustration. After a few moments, Daisy blinked, then looked up at her environment. She left the glasses behind as she approached one of the strawberry bushes, gently pinching one of the little white fruits. "I don't need glasses," she whispered. After she said that, realization seemed to wash over her. "I've been here before."

The beautiful landscape surrounding them slowly grew greyer until its colors were fully muted. The sun was no longer in the sky, which had turned so dark that it was almost black. When Veronica looked back behind them, the glasses were gone without a trace. The leaves on the bushes turned orangish-brown.

"I've had this dream before," Daisy continued. "I'm dreaming."

A few beats passed.

"I know you're there," Daisy said. "Well. I think you're there. I can't see you. But you can see me, can't you?

Veronica's breath caught in her throat. She remained still,

like she was watching a deer she did not want to scare away. The guilt from earlier returned.

"The voice I used to hear is gone. I think it might be...because I killed him in my dream? That sounds insane, I know. It doesn't make any sense. But neither does the voice's sudden disappearance. And *you,* you showed up in my dream the other night." At that point, everything around them was gone. They were floating in a black void. "You know, you're driving me fucking nuts. I don't know what's real anymore. You'd think I'd feel better without the voice, but it only makes me question if it was ever really there at all." She swallowed. "Isn't it a little too precise that it showed up on my eighteenth birthday?" She muttered that last piece. She might have been talking to herself.

Veronica's eyes widened. *Eighteenth birthday?*

"And then it just so happens to disappear the morning after I dream about killing someone? Someone who claimed to *be* the voice? I didn't think too much of it at first, but then I realized something– it didn't even feel like a dream. It was just too *real.* And now you're here. And you're here to take over for him, aren't you? You're the new god, right?" She paused for a few heartbeats and waited for a response, but Veronica could not bring herself to give one. Daisy sighed. "Just come out. I'm tired of talking to the air. Please. I don't want to feel crazy anymore."

A few more moments passed as Veronica changed her settings.

"I didn't mean to make you feel crazy," she replied. Her voice was husky and bashful.

Daisy turned around and faced her. She looked surprised, but only mildly. Quiet simmered between them while Veronica searched for the words to continue her thought.

"I...was trying to make you feel less crazy by appearing to you in your dreams. I mean, what would you have thought if I just showed up in the real world, considering I'd have to make it so you're the only person who can see me? I didn't realize it'd make you feel that way."

"You're really real?"

"Yeah," she mumbled. "But I'm not a god."

"Then what are you?"

"I think you already know. A human. Just a different kind of human from you." She tucked her hands in her pockets.

"Well," Daisy said, stepping closer to Veronica, "Can you watch me whenever you want to?"

"Yes," she admitted. "But– I don't, you know. Watch you all the time, I mean. I have like, an ethical code."

Daisy furrowed her brow and took another step forward. "Can you control my world?"

"I don't," she replied, averting her gaze.

"I didn't ask if you *do* control my world. I asked if you *can*."

"I guess."

They were nose-to-nose. Daisy stared into Veronica's eyes with pointed ferocity. Her stomach churned. *Since when am I intimidated by the Alien Girl? If I'm the one with the power here, why am I so anxious?* Veronica never imagined that their first real interaction would be anything like this. She envisioned herself as the one asking the questions, herself as the one with the upper hand. Not this.

"So you're not a *different kind of human* from me. You're a god. A more hands-off god, albeit, *maybe* more of an altruistic one..."

she looked her up and down. "But a god. And heavy on the *maybe*. You're the one who kidnapped me."

"I didn't know you were real!" Veronica shouted indignantly.

"Sure, but what possessed you to steal from someone so powerful?"

"The greater good is what *possessed* me," Veronica responded, feeling more than a little insulted. "You know what kind of person he is as well as I do. I thought you were just another extension of him, maybe a way for him to spy on other people...I wanted to learn what you *were*. And what I learned was that you weren't an object *at all*. Not like he led us to believe."

"I had a feeling that's what you thought," Daisy whispered under her breath, looking away at last. She bit her thumb, lost in thought. She paced back and forth.

"And by the way," Veronica said, "That vomit was a *bitch* to clean out of my car. Just so you know."

"Who's 'us'?" Daisy asked, ignoring her comment.

"All of us. The entire *world*. Everyone who knew that you existed. We thought that you were just...simple artificial intelligence. Advanced, but still a machine without sentience, regardless. With a realistic mechanical body. Then I tracked down his island and I found his body. And all of the files that he left behind, which I'm sure you looked at too, right?"

"Right."

"Well, after that, I found *your* body. Uh, Eclipta's body, I mean. And..." Gory images bore into her mind again. She shuddered. "I extracted...the technology he used to put you in her body. I kept it safe, then I put you back into your world. So everything must have just felt like a dream to you. I didn't realize it'd make you feel so crazy."

Daisy's expression softened. "So you brought my world back?" she said, her tone soft.

"I guess."

Veronica yelped as she pulled her in for a hug. She didn't hug her back, but Daisy didn't seem to mind.

"Thank you. That's all I wanted whenever I was there. To bring my own world back. That's why I looked through his files in the first place. I thought that he might have something in there about my old universe, maybe how to revive it...but he told me I was from a pocket universe." She pulled away. "And all I learned was that my world wasn't...well, real. He tried to kill me after that, so I killed him, instead. It's a long story."

Veronica didn't reply. They stood in silence for a little while. The black world around them faded to white.

Daisy broke the quiet. "I don't want to feel crazy anymore," she said. "Do you promise that you're real?"

"Yeah."

"I guess that's...kind of a silly thing to ask. How about this. Can you prove that you're real to me?"

Veronica thought for a moment. "Look at your kitchen counter tomorrow," she said. "You'll see something that only I could have done."

"Okay," Daisy replied. After a couple of beats, she added, "See you tomorrow night, okay? Maybe before I go to sleep, this time? Pl-"

Veronica was kicked out of the dream.

Daisy woke up.

—

"...Then she asked me if I could have lunch with her again. It was so weird," Veronica said. "Can you believe it? Where did that even come from?"

Josiah sighed, batting on his turn signal with snarky intention. "You're talkative today, aren't you?"

"She thinks I made time just for her so we could have lunch together."

"How do you know that?"

"Honest to God, Josiah, she *told* me," Veronica said, all too aware of just how excitable of a mood she was in. She allowed herself to indulge in a little zest for once. It was far from unwarranted, given the strides she'd made that day with the Alien Girl. Of course she was in a talkative mood. Still, she found it unfortunate that she couldn't discuss her findings with anyone–Josiah included. "All I said was that it's something I don't ever really have time for, and I just so happened to have time that specific day. Everyone's always so afraid to talk to me, so it was strange...like she wants to be friends with me?"

He clicked his tongue. "You need to be careful."

"What?"

"Veronica, I can very much believe it. I need you to pause and look at it from Nancy's point of view for a second. She might not want to be friends with you. Think about it."

She tried. Hard.

"I don't follow," she said at last.

"Okay. Maybe it's best I explain it to you," he replied, pinching the bridge of his nose. "Wouldn't want you *straining yourself.* It's like this. Let me recount everything you've told me, but from

Nancy's perspective, instead. You're a twenty-one year old, you just got rehired by the same company that you were fired from. It has a new CEO now. Still quite a bit older than you are, but younger than your old boss. Said CEO wants to go to lunch with you after your interview, *and* she pays. She attentively listens to everything you say. When you ask if she wants to do it again sometime, she says that she almost never has time for lunch at all, even by herself..." he raised his eyebrow at Veronica in the rearview mirror. "...Meaning that she made special time just for you. You get it now?"

He looked in the mirror. All he saw was a blank face.

"She thinks you're interested in her."

Veronica screwed up her nose. "Shut up. No she doesn't."

"She totally does," Josiah said. "And if you're not careful, people are going to think that you've got a little scandal going on with one of your employees. I know you're new to having this much power, but this is stuff you have to think about."

"She's too young. She can hardly even legally *drink*. Really? She's a *baby*," Veronica responded.

"Of course you'd want someone who's more experienced with drinking," Josiah muttered.

"You bitch!" she responded. Josiah didn't hear. He was too busy cackling at his own joke. "You know, you're the only person who can get away with saying stuff like that to me."

He settled down after a few more hearty chuckles. His shit-eating grin softened into a warm smile. "It's good to have you back."

—

Waking up was as tough as always. Daisy stretched, then

pressed her palm on her back and popped it into place. She groaned. *I need to save up for a bed, or something,* she thought dully, knowing that she never would. She had that same thought every single morning for as long as she could remember. She'd slept on the couch for years, and it was the most *comforting* spot for her to be, even if it wasn't the most *comfortable.*

She walked to the bathroom, her eyes barely open. A cacophony of joint-cracking echoed through the dusty hallway. She dropped her jaw– she was too lazy to open her mouth with purpose– and began brushing her teeth. Memories from her dream trickled back into her head.

Look at your kitchen counter tomorrow. You'll see something that only I could have done.

Her eyes widened.

With haste, she spit out her toothpaste and all but ran into her kitchen.

An orange rested on her grandma's old wooden cutting board. Next to it was its peel. Daisy picked the rind up and rotated it with the very tips of her fingers. It was intact, lightweight, a perfect sphere– not a single tear was anywhere to be found on its goosebump-ridden surface. Her mouth fell agape.

Her hands shook. She dug her thumbs into the peel and pierced it with her nails once she finished inspecting it.

There was a note inside.

Hi, Daisy! :-)

From, Veronica.

She sat there for a couple of minutes, staring at nothing. Then she vomited into her kitchen sink.

I O

VICE

A second beer, coated with sweat, was wrapped inside Veronica's fingers when she heard a knock at her door. She hid it beneath her desk and began to type on her laptop. All one smooth motion. She'd done it many times before. "Come in," she said. She was lucky that nobody ever dared to burst into her office without knocking first. As quick as she was, she still would have been caught multiple times over by then if not for that.

A blonde head poked its way through the door, soon followed by a pair of doe eyes staring behind thick glasses. "Hey," Nancy said, a bit bashful to be in Veronica's space.

"Hi," she responded dryly. *Fuck, it's her again.* Though Veronica still struggled to believe in Josiah's theories, she still found herself making an effort to seem as disinterested in Nancy as possible. As much as she hated to admit it, seeing how elitist of an idea it was, Veronica was taken aback by the fact that such a low-level employee felt comfortable interrupting her. Especially for no real reason. "I can't do lunch today. Or for a while. I'm very busy."

Nancy blushed. "Oh, that's not...entirely what I came in here for. I just wanted to let you know that...like, Josiah's on his break?"

"It's Wednesday, right?" Veronica responded. "He leaves to take his kids home every Wednesday at three. Nothing new."

"Oh. I didn't know that."

An awkward pause. Veronica kept typing, waiting for Nancy to shut the door and leave, but she didn't. *Why is she still here?*

"Um," Nancy continued, "The bigger thing is that, like, there's a meeting right about now that you put on our schedules. You know. For three? And it's five past three. Are we still on for that...?"

Her fingers froze in place, hovering over the keyboard. *Shit. Why did I set a meeting while Josiah's out? I'm so used to him reminding me of these things, I completely forgot. Fuck. What else did I miss?* She sighed and rubbed her temples. Since she'd rebooted Meta-world, she'd become far more forgetful. She needed to learn how to juggle everything on her plate. "Yeah, we are," she said. "I just got...wrapped up in some things. C'mon. Let's walk together."

Nancy's face lit up. Veronica cringed. *"Let's walk together"? Be careful, dumbass.*

As they strolled down the hallway, Veronica snuck a couple of glances at Nancy and realized that Josiah was probably right. She was staring at her like a lovesick puppy. She decided that she had to confront it. "Nancy," she said, "you're a hard worker.

Thank you for being such an integral part of Axis." *That should do it. You can't get more professionally distant than that.*

The expression on Nancy's face only deepened. Veronica tried not to groan.

ROOM RESERVED: MEETING: THE FUTURE OF AXIS, the digital plaque next to the west conference room's entryway read. Veronica planned to talk about projections, potential investments, and how they planned to expand their scope. All employees intermediate-level and above were required to attend. Since the billionaire had these same "future meetings" every month or so, Veronica thought that there was worth in continuing them— even if it was really just to help the employees retain a sense of normalcy and routine. It was one of those harmless things he did that she didn't mind keeping, even if she found it somewhat unnecessary.

When she walked through the door, hundreds of eyes burned into her. She tried to ignore her own shame over arriving a few minutes late, but she failed. It didn't help that she arrived with Nancy. Anxiety gnawed at her as she took the microphone off its stand– that, at least, had been prepared for her. Did Nancy say anything about her infatuation with Veronica to her coworkers? Did it seem suspicious that they walked in side-by-side? Did she sense a tad of judgment in her audience's aura?

They're waiting for you to say something. Come on.

She swallowed hard. "I'm pleased to see that so many of you could make it today," she said. "I apologize for my tardiness. I've been wrapped up in my work."

The room remained silent.

"With that out of the way, let's get started. In order to

continue the spirit of discussion that this company has so successfully fostered before my promotion, I want this to function as somewhat of a loose Socratic seminar. Everyone in this room will be allowed to share their visions. Allow me to start off—we're looking to expand Axis in ways that have never been seen before. I've been scouring recent scientific publications to find ways to optimize and upgrade our systems. I've also been seeking out ways to come up with entirely new systems. My research has included *all* scientific or science-adjacent fields, by the way—never just what we think of as conventional computer science. Linguistics, biochemistry, astronomy, psychology, sociology..." She paced back and forth at the front of the room and spoke with her hands, just like how the billionaire used to do. She thought it might make herself seem more familiar and authentic to them, even if she always found it reminiscent of a frat boy pumping himself up to do a keg stand when the billionaire did it. "We can never stay self-referential in our field. We need to find new and creative ways to use any kind of science we can get our hands on to make something that is truly fresh. Find inspiration in the unconventional. Act as artists, because that is exactly what we are. This is a room full of incredibly intelligent folks, and I've seen it first hand. I have good faith in this team. You know that, how about you give yourselves a round of applause before we continue? Let's hear it!"

The room didn't explode the way Veronica imagined it would. The crowd kept their applause reserved, not seeming to take their eyes off of her. She'd ad-libbed that line to try and put the crowd and herself at ease, but she only felt more nervous. *What's wrong with me? Has the interview really set me this far back in public speaking?*

Or am I just disliked?

She waited for them to finish applauding, then continued. "We all know that tech can be used for both good and evil. Here at Axis, we're in the business of using powerful technology for the greater good above all else. Before I share my own ideas, I want to hear from you. What would make your life easier? What would improve society overall? How would you go about it? The question I'm really asking, folks, is *what would make the world a better place?*"

She walked around the room and scanned the audience for a raised hand. Not so much as a murmur broke the lone sound of her heels clicking against steps. Her nerves lit up like a circuit board. She was relieved when, after some hesitation, a hand stuck out amidst the crowd. As she approached it, she noticed that it belonged to a young man, probably about Nancy's age. He wore a powder blue t-shirt and jeans. Thick chestnut hair cascaded down his shoulders. He had intimidating icy eyes. She passed the microphone down to him.

"I think that we should focus on the fact that we have technology now that prevents elements from decaying. We could definitely use that to develop some powerful things."

Veronica mustered a smile and pressed the microphone back to her own lips. "I've been thinking about the same exact thing. You know, my team used that technology ourselves, once upon a time. We were trying to develop a new line of computers, and we ended up with some cool components. Mostly processors. Too bad it was canceled...perhaps we could revisit that soon."

He stared off into space as he measured her words, deep in thought. Veronica found another hand stretching over the vast sea of employees.

"Maybe we could revisit it in a different way," the young woman said. "A machine that prevents elements from decaying could prevent data rot, entirely. Maybe we could make a machine that sort of incubates data. Or there might be more money in just making a proprietary line of data storage units–"

"We can do better than that," someone called out from across the room. Both Veronica and the woman whipped their heads around, surprised by the interruption. "We need to use that tech for its most obvious purpose. In this day and age, we need to get into developing real weaponry. I believe that everyone in this room together could figure out how to upgrade the B132. We have the connections, we have the means, we have the security, and we have the demand from the Californian government. The U.S. has the B132, and the R.O.C. would kill for something bigger. *That's* what we'll make money from. That's how we'll make the world a better place. By supporting our country.

Veronica froze. *Make the world a better place?*

The room went quiet for a heartbeat. Some of the employees started murmuring to one another in agreement. Then, all at once, they swelled into full-blown discussion, everyone's voices overlapping. Some seemed cautious, but many seemed to be in agreement. Veronica felt like a deer in headlights. She looked over at Nancy, who was sitting in the front row. She kept silent among the chatter. Veronica shoved the microphone toward her.

"Supervise this," she hissed. "I have to leave. Something's come up."

Nancy blinked, confused. Regardless, she nodded.

As Veronica walked out of the room, she was vaguely aware of Nancy's awkward voice echoing through the hallways, explaining that she had to leave early. She didn't care. She needed to be out of there.

She headed straight for Metaworld.

—

"What time is it in your world?"

"About four o'clock."

"You're here early."

"I know, I know. I needed...an escape from something."

"I understand. Trust me."

Daisy sat on her couch, staring up at Veronica with wide eyes. Her grandmother was out shopping. Veronica, awkward and gangly in stature compared to Daisy, stood with her thumbs jammed in her pockets. She was looking around the living room, half to avoid eye contact and half out of curiosity. She didn't realize how small the rooms in Metaworld were until she stood in the middle of one. Then again, the people there were significantly shorter than her. When they were both standing, Veronica stood a solid foot taller than Daisy. However, Veronica was on the taller side in her own world, as well, so she wasn't sure how accurate her own perception of Metaworld residents' height was. She picked up a porcelain figurine, observed the little painted details on its surface, then put it back down.

"I have to be honest," Daisy said, "I appreciate the evidence you left out for me, but..." she trailed off. "Nevermind."

"But what?" Veronica prompted.

"But it's kind of disturbing. It almost made me feel...more crazy."

Veronica couldn't help but let out an exasperated sigh.

"I know, I know. That's what I asked for. But, like...well, you had a point about how appearing in my dreams is a little less threatening than showing up in person."

"What a surprise," she sing-songed sarcastically.

Daisy scrunched up her face. "Okay, well, you know what? It still sucked for you to hang out in my dreams like that. It *still* made me feel crazy." She paused. "*Makes* me feel crazy."

She quirked an eyebrow. "All you need to do is show me to someone else. If someone else can see me, then that proves you're not crazy. Why not introduce me to your *grandmother?*" She accidentally mimicked Daisy's voice on the word "grandmother" in an impulsive flash of bitterness, but she did not feel apologetic about it.

"You're fucking nuts," Daisy shot back. "Like hell I'm introducing *you* to my grandmother." She sniffed and lifted her chin in contempt.

"What?" Veronica asked. "I'm not a nice enough girl to bring home to your family?"

Daisy's face pinkened. "You *know why.* 'Hi, this is Veronica. She came here from a different universe, by the way. Can she crash on our couch?' Don't be a dick."

Veronica couldn't help but crack a smirk at how indignant she'd made her. *Like a snarly chihuahua.* "What, you can't just lie to her?"

Her tone grew solemn. "No. I can't."

Potent silence permeated between them for a moment.

Veronica got the feeling that she shouldn't unravel that thread any further.

"Any other ideas? I mean, I'm here to help," she added after a couple more heartbeats.

Daisy deliberated for a moment, then her face lit up. "Do you like clubbing?"

"What?"

"Do you want to go clubbing with me? Listen, I was planning on going out tonight, anyway. You could come with me. Then I'll know that other people can see you. I won't have to lie to anyone, because I don't know anyone there well enough for them to question why you're there with me."

Veronica thought about it. She hadn't been out to so much as a party since she was much younger, and she'd never been clubbing at all. From what she saw on TV, all you had to do was get dressed and dance. Or something. *God. I'm a loser.* Maybe it was worth trying out– how many people could say that they did such a thing in a different universe? Not that she'd be able to say anything about it, herself– but it'd be an experience, for sure.

"Okay," she responded. "I'll go clubbing with you tonight. And you promise it'll make you feel less crazy?"

Daisy grinned. "Probably. No guarantee."

11

OPTICS

For both women, it was a strange feeling getting ready for a night out next to someone they hardly knew. Or getting ready next to anyone at all, for that matter. Among the many options available to Veronica was a way to customize her body any way she liked, which saved her the awkwardness of choosing between having to borrow a too-short outfit from Daisy, going out shopping somewhere in Metaworld that wouldn't have her size, or wearing the bland default clothing she already had on. After typing several prompts, tweaking each one a little from the last, she ended up with an outfit that she might have worn in her own universe. She donned something just as sleek as the world she came from. It was geometric and smooth. It was an asymmetrical black dress with a strange, large hair piece made of different basic shapes. Perfectly chaotic squares and triangles popped out of her hair. Not quite what she was going for– maybe a little more feminine than she would have liked– but it would do just fine. For the sake of camaraderie, she'd borrowed some of Daisy's eyeliner and glitter eyeshadow. Daisy couldn't help but stare.

"What?" Veronica asked self-consciously. She lowered the makeup applicator.

"You kind of look like a foreign model."

Veronica clutched her stomach in laughter. She almost stumbled out of the tall heels she'd decided to wear. "*How?* This is just something I threw together."

"Really?" Daisy asked. "Nobody wears anything like that here. It's so..."

Veronica's face fell. "Should I change?"

"No," Daisy continued. Her tone was amicable. "It's so fashion-forward. Like, it's progressive. Think about it. You're so tall already, and you've got those heels on, too...you've got the big eyes, the high cheekbones, this outfit–"

Veronica quirked an eyebrow.

"You look great, is what I'm trying to say. You're going to draw attention. Which is good!"

"I didn't know this expedition was for *fun,* or I would have worn something a little more fashionable than this," Veronica replied. "I thought we were just proving that I'm not a hallucination."

More fashionable? There's outfits more fashion-forward than what she's wearing? Daisy thought. She looked down at her own strapless red dress and felt a little plain next to Veronica. "We are. Can't it be both?"

"Sure," Veronica said. "Just don't run off where I can't find you. Girl code and all that."

"*Girl code.* You guys have a term for that too?" Daisy started laughing. "Is clubbing etiquette universal?"

Veronica smiled. "I guess that it is. What do you all call it?" She flicked Daisy's eyeliner pen across her face, producing a long, thick wing. That was something she learned back in middle school. *Thank God for the permanence of muscle memory.*

"Rules of sisterhood," Daisy replied. "Rules women follow when they go out together. Right? Yours rolls of the tongue better than ours, though."

"Yeah," Veronica replied, intentionally vague as to which part she was agreeing with. Her mouth fell open while she finished applying her makeup. Then she stood up straight and hiked up her dress straps, adjusting her breasts in place. "I wouldn't usually dress like this. It's kind of fun."

"Why did you dress like that *this* time? How do you usually dress?" Daisy asked as they walked out the door. She locked it behind them, then they paced toward the elevator.

"Different universe, different style? Something like that? I mean, this is a whole new world, and I can experiment a little bit. You know? Usually, I'd wear a suit."

"I would've liked to see you in a suit," Daisy replied. She blushed and screwed her mouth shut as soon as the words came out of her mouth. Veronica only chuckled in response. She didn't seem to pick up on Daisy's embarrassment.

"Oh, I wear a suit *every day.* I'm sure you will. I don't wear makeup either, but I suppose it's nice to feel glamorous every once in a while."

They stepped out of the apartment's lobby. When she finished her sentence, Veronica peered up above her and noticed the gorgeous dark teal sky blanketing the atmosphere. Her eyes widened. *Like something out of a vintage anime.* Fat cotton candy clouds sleepily coasted along the gentle breeze. It swept across Veronica's lips, which were slightly parted in amazement. It tasted sweet and woody. Dim, sienna-toned street lights illuminated cobblestone paths– a stark contrast to the smooth broken sidewalks in her own version of the world. Her heart tightened. she thought about the meeting she'd hosted earlier. Her own employees wanted to develop weaponry that could destroy their entire planet, weaponry that was somehow worse and more torturous than permanently disabling people and destroying their homes. Worse than forcibly sterilizing the majority of a country's population, leaving them in chronic pain, forcing them to seek refuge in self-serving, disgustingly capitalist places that never wanted them there in the first place. So much was going on in her own universe, she didn't know what to do with all of the stress it imposed on her. The pressure to be just as self-serving and awful as every other person of her status, emphasized with the threat of the U.S. government *and* the R.O.C., the labels thrust upon her, the way that she was treated because she was a Black woman and an immigrant, a descendent of Colombians, even though she knew absolutely nothing about her family that far back and could hardly even remember moving to the U.S. as a small child–

"Hey. We're here," Daisy said. She lightly brushed her fingers against Veronica's shoulder.

"Oh," she responded. "Sorry. I got like, wrapped up in my own thoughts–"

"It's okay. I do that too, sometimes." Daisy offered her a sheepish grin. "Let's both help ourselves feel less crazy. Alright?"

Veronica could already feel the pulsating music beating inside of her chest like a drum. Someone stepped out of the club. She glanced inside. The noise opened up with the door. Laughter, chatter, and bassy music thumped out of the entryway. It was unlike anything she'd ever heard before, but she recognized the sound as something reminiscent of EDM. She imagined that a world that was essentially living in her own world's 1990s when it came to tech would be more acoustic-leaning. It almost sounded like her own world's experimental music, with its odd time signatures and strange instrumentation...it was repetitive, but not in the same way the music she knew of was repetitive. Above all, it was fast-paced. She liked it.

"Anything I should know before we go in there?" she asked Daisy.

"If someone asks you if you want some candy, don't take it."

Veronica howled. "*No way.* You guys do that here, too? When people go to raves in my world, they like to put their stuff in Skittle boxes."

"What's a Skittle?"

Veronica laughed even harder. She decided to put everything about her own world out of her mind for once.

The music was overwhelming, just as she expected it to be. Veronica could not pick a single voice out of the crowd. Flashing lights flooded the floor, hues of green and pink and purple, all spinning across the dark industrial room. Come to think of it, the place looked like a repurposed old warehouse. The only static light source came from rows of light blue lamps hanging above the bar, an oasis in the middle of the madness. Her head stuck out like a lone sunflower in a field of tulips. Veronica was tempted to crouch down to their level and lose herself in the crowd. Daisy seemed to manage doing exactly that just fine. *How?* But after she remembered how Daisy compared her to a foreign model, she decided to try and embrace her stature. Not much else she could do about it, after all. A few people were staring, Veronica noticed. Not in a bad way. She still felt awkward. What if they didn't like her dancing? They merely seemed curious, but what if that curiosity turned to ridicule after they watched her for long enough? It wasn't a matter of *if* she would commit a faux pas of some kind, it was a matter of *when*. She'd rather if they didn't look at her at all. *I shouldn't have come here. I should have found another way to–*

Daisy interrupted her thought by wrapping her hand around Veronica's wrist. She looked down. The shorter woman's lips were moving, but she could not hear a single word coming out of her mouth.

"What?" she shouted, leaning down. She cupped one hand around her ear and used the other to keep her dress pulled over her thighs.

"I said, how did you peel that orange anyway?" she repeated. Directly in her ear, this time.

"Oh. I just, like, took it out."

"Yeah, but how?"

"You know. Like. How you would take anything out of anything. Like...like how you could lift a pig out of a pen without ever opening the gate? You know?"

"No. I don't know. Who the fuck is strong enough to lift a pig out of a pen?"

Veronica leaned back and cackled at Daisy's stupid half-joke, if it was even meant to be a joke at all. She clapped her hands as she laughed. "Shut up," she replied once she caught her breath. Daisy joined in, both women mute underneath the music's thick vibrations. Then she began to dance, disregarding her thoughts from earlier. Neither of them had a single drop of alcohol in their body, but they still felt intoxicated, in love with their surroundings, living in the moment.

Her eyes traveled back over to Daisy, who was still hanging on to the laughter they shared. For a moment, everything moved in slow motion. A spotlight swiveled across Daisy and illuminated her back. It silhouetted her body with a perfect bright pink halo while everyone else was still colored with shades of blue and violet. As she stretched her neck way back, her head thrusting backwards in ecstasy, her eyes flashed, brightened by a radiant burst of white from the lights above. Her spine curved into a perfect half-backbend. *The golden ratio.* She looked just like a painting. Breathless, Veronica couldn't help but stare.

Just as soon as the moment began, it was over. Daisy threw herself forward and grabbed Veronica's hands. She almost tripped into her. Veronica caught her and pushed her upright.

"I'm so glad you're real," she said, her tone rife with the leftovers of a giggle. She paid no mind to her own stumble. "You're *killing it.* Look. They can *see* you! God, I'm so relieved."

Veronica surveyed the area. Though she was dizzy from her own feverish dancing and belly-deep laughter, she could still tell that people were looking at her. They'd made a small clearing around her, clapping and cheering her on.

"Wow," she lamely offered. She looked back down at Daisy. "What if...what if all of this is a hallucination, though? Then...what?" She teased, out of breath. When Daisy's face fell, she was hit with instant regret. *Fuck. Bad joke to make. I'm so dumb.*

She was surprised when Daisy's smile returned a moment later. "I don't care what's real anymore, either way," she said earnestly, clutching Veronica's shoulders. "I'm happy."

12

GONE

Veronica all but sprinted toward the back seat of the car. She was about two hours late. She was surprised that Josiah was still waiting for her at all– she thought that she might have to find a ride herself. When she checked her phone after leaving Meta-world, her lock screen's notifications documented that he'd tried to call her 23 times. She imagined that he would be pissed, to say the least. She couldn't check how he was feeling by looking through the car windows, since they were tinted so dark. That only made her more anxious.

Her hunch was right. Josiah was still and firm, jaw clenched, his arms crossed. Unblinking eyes looked at her in the rearview mirror. A nervous smile spread across her face. She felt like a child who was about to receive a scolding.

"Heard you had an interesting day."

"Well. Yeah. Uh, I got...wrapped up in some stuff."

"What kind of stuff?" Josiah tapped his fingers on his arm. "What are you keeping from me?

"Nothi–" Veronica started. The last part of her sentence slipped away when he lifted his hand, snapped it shut, and clicked his tongue. For a moment, the only sound that could be heard was the car motor's soft hum.

"You walk out in the middle of a meeting that you were late to, you straight up *disappear* on everyone. I can't find you *any-where* when I come back from dropping off my kids, who, by the way, are stuck at home right now. Waiting for me to bring them dinner, because clearly I'm not going to have time to cook tonight. So don't tell me that it's *nothing*. It's not nothing. It's your future, your image, and honestly? It's our friendship, too. I thought we were friends."

"Listen," Veronica said. "I'm sorry, okay? Seriously. I lost track of time. I..." she trailed off. "I can't tell you any more than that. I'm sorry."

"Why not?" He narrowed his eyes.

"It's just...stuff that I can't get you wrapped up in."

"Seriously? Of all the things we've done together, *this* is what you can't tell me?"

"Josiah, I promise you that it is something..." she trailed off. "I can't discuss it here, anyway. And I can't discuss it with you, not because I don't trust you. It's just not safe. I'm sitting on stuff that the government would *kill* for. Governments, plural, actually. Both the R.O.C. and the U.S.A., either one, take your damn pick. You wanna talk about image? Look at me, I'm target number one. I'm a 'dirty socialist' just because I don't want to be a fucking billionaire and I pay my employees a living wage.

Just in case you haven't fucking noticed, I'm Black, I come from a family of immigrants, of Colombians, who I haven't even met, by the way, I'm a woman, and I've got more eyes on me than ever. I'm running the biggest fucking company this side of the world. Do you think that's fun? Because it's not! You don't really get what it's like, to be the person I am in the position I'm in." She felt herself growing more frustrated by the second. "And I'm not ever, *ever* allowed to complain. Above everything else."

"I don't understand what that's like," Josiah said. "I know that. But Veronica, when was the last time you asked me about *my* life? Or about *anyone's* life? I feel like you're always the topic of conversation. I *know* you have a lot going on, but it's always all about you. Selectively, too. Because I guess you like to keep secrets now."

"It's for your own good, Josiah. You have a family to take care of," Veronica whispered.

He snapped. "Since when do you care about what's good for me, *Xanthippe?*"

"Don't call me that anymore," Veronica whispered. Josiah ignored her.

"To you, I'm just a means to get yourself around, to vent about your past, like you don't damn well know how I've lost and grieved and hurt and busted my ass just as you have, to remember your *own goddamn meetings* that you're just going to abandon anyway to run around and do *whatever you do–* or *whoever* you do, I mean, I didn't see *Nancy* anywhere when I came back– and no matter how long that takes you, you take it for granted that I'm going to be here in the end. You're right, Veronica, I do have a family to go home to and tend to, not like you'd know what that's like." As soon as the last sentence exited his lips, he covered his mouth.

Veronica stared at him, her brow furrowed.

"Veronica. I didn't mean–"

She unbuckled her seatbelt and threw the car door open. "Don't worry about picking me up and dropping me off anymore," she hissed. Then, without looking back, she strode back toward the lab.

—

A heavy grunt escaped her as she finished moving the last piece of furniture– Alien Girl's cot– into the room that housed Metaworld. She was misted with sweat from wheeling all of the units out of the way to make space for her living area. It was a hodge-podge of old, plain items. All of it was found exclusively in the laboratory's abandoned wing. A surprisingly thin layer of dust was the only evidence that all of the furniture had remained untouched for so long. *So sterile in here,* she thought.

She put her hands on her hips and surveyed the room. It looked bare, but perfectly acceptable. *I'll just start sleeping here at night. I'll rent a moving van tomorrow... Start living out of the laboratory. Like* he *did. The lease on my apartment is up soon, anyway...Bratty should be good on food for tonight...I can sleep in my clothes for now, use the Alien Girl's old bathroom...*

Her face contorted. She stumbled to the side of her bed and dropped to her knees. Hot tears slid down her cheeks. Small, pain-laden choked sobs erupted from her throat. She knew that Josiah didn't mean the full implications of what he'd said to her. It didn't make it hurt any less. The meeting from earlier turned that sore spot into an especially raw wound. Veronica knew nothing about her own culture, nor did she know anything about her own flesh and blood that must have either been dead or living in unimaginable pain right at that moment. Her own employees wanted to create a weapon even worse than the one that destroyed her mother's culture– no, *her* culture– to near unrecognizable lengths. She was almost grateful that her mother passed away before she ever could have seen just how terrible the world had become. She was just a child when her mother died. She was just a child when the Bogotá Testing Incident happened, and she was just a child when the world accused Colombia of "stealing" the B132, using it against its own citizens, and framing the United States.

She lay flat on the cot. The tears streaming down her face soaked into the flat yellow pillow beneath her like a sponge. She had only one family member left, and she hadn't spoken to him in months. Her own father. He never asked to be a dad in the first place, and though he tried to convince Veronica that she was loved and wanted, the fact that he never fully accepted his role as her father was abundantly clear. The one person who ever truly wanted her was her mom. She wished it was easier to remember all of the good things about being her mother's child. Veronica was just so small when she died.

She shut her eyes and recalled the last time she'd gone home to see her dad. It was hard to imagine why she thought it was a good idea to visit. At the time, she supposed, it felt like some kind of rite of passage to go home to visit what little family she had and celebrate. It was right after she inherited the company. A vision of her father, pudgy and awkward, too-big for the cheap little futon he sat on, came to her. She sat on his recliner and leaned toward him, hands folded as if it were a job interview. It was so nerve-wracking, being there.

"I remember when you were just a tiny little ankle-biter," her dad said, breaking a long silence between the two of them. It was only interrupted by the sound of ice clinking against glass every once in a while. He clutched a glass of vodka in one strong hand, resting it on the arm of the couch. It was the first thing he said to her outside of small talk. Perhaps the alcohol helped him brave an actual conversation. "And I just...didn't know what to do with you." His eyes glazed over. She wasn't sure if he was getting emotional or just zoning out from reliving old memories.

"I mean, here was this...here's this mini human that *I* helped produce, and I can't even understand her." He chuckled. "You only spoke *French.* My own daughter, and it's like she's from a completely different world. It was incredible. It was terrifying."

Veronica blinked. "I don't remember speaking French."

"Of course you don't. Do you speak any French *now*?"

Veronica looked at the floor. "Uh. Not at all."

Her father grinned at her. "And that's entirely my fault. I wish I could have nurtured that instead of...forcing English on you, you know? I wish I could have taught you both. Ah, well. Look where you are now, anyway. Didn't hold you back *that* much, don't you think? Do you want something to drink?" He was already sloshed.

Veronica shook her head.

"And, you know," he grunted, hoisting himself up from his chair, "Sometimes...love is so weird. I tried to learn French for your mother, but I just couldn't pick it up, especially not over one summer. And you know what else, Ronnie, sometimes...sometimes people grow *apart*. And that, well, it's just A-OK. Your mother was a *fantastic* woman. A wonderful person, a wonderful friend. But did that mean we were right for one another as more than friends? Nah...but hey, we made a hell of a fling." He laughed loudly, clutching his stomach. Veronica's eyes followed him as he made his way to his minifridge. He took out a can of beer and tossed it to her. "Come on," he said, "I know you love 'em."

She caught it rather ungracefully and stared at the label for a heartbeat. She glanced back at her dad. He looked expectant. Without another word, she cracked it open and pressed it to her lips.

"Atta girl."

They never spoke about what happened *before* she moved to the United States. It was ironic. They were bonded by it, in a twisted sort of way. In a complete freak accident, her mother slipped off a stepladder. When she was old enough, Veronica learned that her neck snapped upon impact with the hard linoleum floor. She died instantly. But as a small child, she had no way of knowing that. All she knew was that she needed to get in contact with someone. Panicking, she slipped her mother's phone off the kitchen counter. Veronica couldn't read anything on the screen. She didn't know how yet; she was too young. Lucky for her, her mother added emojis to all of her contacts. A briefcase for her boss, a pizza slice for their favorite restaurant, the like. Veronica's father got a sunflower. It was recognizable. A young Veronica remembered all of the times her mother video called that nice man she got to talk to sometimes by pressing the name with the sunflower emoji. She didn't recognize him as her father. Her mother never *called* him that. To her, he was just their friend. She would come to learn that it was a mutual agreement. Veronica's mom loved having a daughter all to her own, so she didn't mind that the man she was pregnant by wasn't ready to be a parent. In fact, maybe she preferred it that way. Veronica was fine with it, too. But it just wasn't the way that things stayed.

Veronica still couldn't remember speaking a single word of French, but she did remember that she could not understand a word coming out of that man's mouth. After failing to get any-where through a frantic back-and-forth, she pointed the camera at her mother's body. Then everything happened. She was taken away by a group of big adults, she was questioned in a bare-white room, and she was taken to the United States. For a while, she wondered where her mother went. It took a long time for her to realize that she would not ever be back to come and get her. And at last, that nice man stepped up and became her father, as ill-equipped as he was. She wondered all the time about what her life would have been like if her mother never died.

She wished she didn't feel so resentful about it. She knew that he tried his best.

Veronica's mind made its way back to how that conversation ended.

"You know, Dad," she said, "I don't really get how you and mom..." she trailed off. "I mean, you video called, you were to-gether for a whole summer, you never spoke the same language."

Her dad looked up at the ceiling and tapped his chin. "Well," he started, "we had translator apps, you know, when it was im-portant..." he sighed. "There were so few things that mattered to us, and I guess speaking the same language wasn't one of them."

Dad, she wanted to ask next, *why a sunflower emoji?* She never did.

13

ECHO

Veronica did everything she could to make herself look as presentable as possible the following morning. It was difficult, considering that she didn't get any sleep and was missing a decent change of clothes, but she supposed that she wouldn't have anything to worry about for *too* long. Soon enough, she'd have everything she needed. She'd already hired movers. They'd show up soon to pick up her key. Having a stupid amount of money had its benefits, she supposed, and she still didn't make nearly as much as the billionaire. What did he *do* with all of it?

She trudged her way out the door like a fatigued teenager. Dread filled her chest when she thought about how awkward it would be to see Josiah again.

What she didn't realize was that he'd be waiting for her as soon as she opened the door.

"Veronica," he said dryly.

"What are you doing here?" she rasped. He really sought out where she'd been staying? Her walls were back up in an instant. "I don't want an apology from you. I want you to leave me–"

"It's not about that," he interrupted. His voice was stone cold. "We need to talk. In your office, preferably. Now."

—

She seethed the entire way there. Josiah did not look over at her a single time. At least, not from what she could see through the angry glances she kept sneaking. Hurt glances, in actuality. He didn't say a word the whole way there.

As soon as she walked through the doorway and shut the door behind her, she whipped around to look at Josiah. "What do you need to tell me," she deadpanned.

"There's been a data breach," he replied, returning her annoyed cadence. She tried not to let her expression change, but her organs swirled inside of her. She took some time before she responded to calm down. Her voice still could not help but betray some of her worry– her words came out shaky. "Okay. How was it done? What's been compromised?"

"It was completed remotely. And I don't know yet."

"That's not possible. We have some of the best systems in the entire world. Who could have done it?"

The corner of Josiah's mouth twitched. "Don't know. Maybe it was someone like you, back when you were younger...some plucky teen savant who wanted to see what would happen. Maybe it was an organization far more powerful and malicious than that. Based on the way it was executed, I don't think it was one of our employees. Whoever it was, they definitely know what they're doing. I haven't found anything that points to a single specific culprit yet."

Veronica dropped her head into the palms of her hands. She couldn't believe what was happening. "But I have security *leagues* above what anyone has ever seen or developed before," she said. She stopped bothering to mask her voice. Anxiety seeped its way into her tone. She was vulnerable again.

Josiah did not change his manner of speaking. "And you don't think that makes you a more enticing target? No matter how good you are, there's always someone who's better. Or some *ones*. Every system has its vulnerabilities, and one of ours has been found."

Veronica opened her mouth to speak again, to ask Josiah if he had an idea of where the vulnerability was, if it had been patched yet, but she was interrupted by an uncomfortable presence. Someone shuffled behind them. She and Josiah whipped around at the same time. Nancy was shyly lingering in the doorway, looking as if she were about to sneak back out.

"Nancy," Josiah said, exasperated, "How much did you hear?"

Veronica felt like kicking herself for forgetting to lock her door. Since when was she so bad at security?

There was a pause before Veronica exploded. "Give me one good reason why I shouldn't send your ass packing right now."

Nancy's eyes widened to the size of saucers and became glossy. Her bottom lip quivered.

"*Veronica*," Josiah hissed.

She stood her ground. She stared down at Nancy, who looked like she was about to cry. She looked back over at Josiah. He was meeting her gaze with the stern air of a disappointed father.

After a few seconds, something about the tension squared her back into reality.

"Fuck," she whispered, turning away from them both. She felt as if she were about to start crying herself.

"Am I really fired?" Nancy squeaked. Her face was high-lighter pink.

"No, Nancy," Veronica responded. "Just...go. Don't tell anyone about anything you heard today. You got me?"

She nodded and shuffled out of the room, covering her face with her hands. As she left, Veronica was hit with a wave of guilt. Her own outburst reminded her all too much of her predecessor.

Josiah turned back toward Veronica. Something told her that if it wasn't for more pressing matters, he'd be tearing into her right then. But he didn't. He debriefed her rapid-fire, answering every question racing through her mind quicker than she could think them up. That was something he was very skilled at. "We need to patch it up now. I traced the vulnerability back to the software associated with some of the projects you mentioned from the island. It shouldn't take too long, and it should be a relatively easy fix, too...there must have been an oversight when you were going over his old projects. Veronica, you really should have left it to the cybersecurity specialists–"

"I *am* a cybersecurity specialist. Aside from engineering, that's *what I do best*. You *know* that."

Josiah pinched the bridge of his nose. "But it's not your *job*. You used to be head engineer, now you're the head of the entire company. Neither of those roles require as much involvement in cybersecurity as you insist on having. Running Axis doesn't mean you can just do everything *yourself* like you seem to believe– the opposite.You have a lot on your plate, you need to focus on what you–" he interrupted himself and sighed. "I'm not going to argue with you right now."

"Good." Veronica indulged in her own snideness. Her stomach felt like it was full of stones, and she was trying not to show how shaky she was feeling. *A vulnerability in the projects on the island? Is Daisy safe?* Though she was able to stay level-headed the worst of times, she felt as if she were about to start panicking.

"*Anyway*," Josiah continued, "We need to get to work ASAP. Where did he develop all of his island projects? Do you know? I can tell that the vulnerability is local, so it must be somewhere in this buildi-"

Veronica dropped the curt veneer just as soon as it came. She sighed and showed him her palm, a gesture that was part interruption and part admission of defeat. "Yeah," she rasped. "Follow me. Back where we came from."

—

An awkward tension collected between them when they entered Veronica's new room. It was already cluttered in a way that made it obvious it was lived in. They both side-eyed one another at the same time. Josiah squinted at the scene with parted lips, his eyebrow furrowed in mild confusion. When he noticed the look on her face, guilty and pleading, she watched it all click for him in real time. It only deepened her hangdog expression.

"You're sleeping here," he said, half question, half statement.

Veronica looked away from him and shrugged her shoulders.

"I mean...why?" he sputtered. "Really? You're so married to your work, you have to *live* here?"

Veronica's eyes lowered. "I *told* you that you don't have to worry about picking me up anymore."

Josiah's face flushed and pinched together. She would have thought it was funny if they weren't in the middle of a heated argument. "No, you're not pinning this on *me*. This was inevitable. You would have ended up living here either way, let's be honest."

Because she knew that he was right, she changed the subject. Veronica already felt about as ashamed as she could handle right then. Her worst traits were on full display, all right in front of Josiah to be tinkered with and pulled apart and criticized– but more importantly, they were right in front of *herself.* She loathed those reminders of her own obsessive hard-headedness. "I don't have time for this," she said. "*We* don't have time for this. We need to get moving."

He didn't say another word. Veronica paced toward the monitor, a sleek centerpiece to the strange beauty of all of the united and plain furniture splayed across the room, then tensed up. Project Metaworld was an endlessly running program. As soon as she turned that screen on and entered her password, Josiah would be able to see Daisy. *Daisy* would be able to perceive Veronica, too. Interact with her. After all, she never turned the perception toggle back off. She paused.

"What are you waiting for?" Josiah said, his tone steeped in annoyance. "*Now* what?"

"I need you to get out," Veronica said.

"*What?*"

"That's an order," she continued, turning to look at him. The worried sickness in her body spilled out through her voice. Her tone was flat. Dead. Upon seeing her wide, pink-rimmed eyes, he pursed his lips together in suspicion. Then he nodded, and with some hesitance, he made his way back out of the room. Veronica could not bring herself to care about the fact that she'd only reinforced his mistrust, and she didn't have time to dress herself up with niceties. She would worry about that later. For then, she needed to take action, and that was exactly what she was going to do.

She opened Metaworld as soon as she heard the door click behind her. The screen was centered on Daisy's perspective, as always. Before she had a chance to acknowledge Veronica's presence with anything more than an excited smile, she began speaking.

"Daisy," she whispered into the computer's microphone, "I have to do something real fast. Right now. Just hang tight. Okay? You're not going to feel like anything's happened at all."

Daisy's smile fell. She looked bewildered, but she nodded.

Veronica quit the program and navigated to the system's menu. She shut down every server in the building until none were online. Next, she opened the system's file directory. Some of the files had names that matched up with the files on the island. While she was at it, she hid Metaworld's folder using password protection. Soon, no sign of Metaworld's existence could be found anywhere– at least, not on the surface. That would protect it from prying eyes, whether they belonged to a hacker or anyone else.

With meticulous precision, she checked every possible entry point in the system. The tedious work made it so she couldn't help but let her mind wander from the task at hand. She couldn't help but wonder how the person who breached the system even knew about it in the first place, let alone accessed it. Yes, it was easy to believe that there was a simple oversight when she updated the billionaire's systems. Sure. But she was so *thorough*. Especially with a fully isolated network containing information as sensitive as that. How was it done by someone outside the company? It wasn't possible. She couldn't believe it. It made her feel insane. Why now? Why *after* the security had been upgraded so heavily? Why not access this information back when her old boss was still alive– back when it could have been done through a fucking phishing email, so long as it was sent to the right person?

Realization hit her like a truck. Her head snapped up. She stared at the floor, her vision swimming and mouth agape. She forced it back shut only when she began to drool all over the tile as if she were about to vomit.

Furious determination flooded her chest. She began combing through the system with newfound purpose. Whoever was accessing their network must have been forcibly booted out of it when she disconnected from the internet, but she still felt like there was someone watching her every move. Breathing down her neck. Waiting like a ghost haunting the computer.

After a long and frantic search, thick silence only broken by the hot low breath of the computer's ventilation and the rhythm of pressed keycaps, she found what she was looking for. Her suspicions were right. As Josiah stated, the billionaire failed to make his system, created specifically to house all of his secrets about his weird pet project, air-tight. That part was obvious. But as far as she knew, there was only one point of entry to the system that could have been exploited, and it could only have been exploited by one type of entity. She scanned the network's security log and found that foreign code had been injected into Axis's private servers.

One of these things is not like the others.

It was downloaded exactly one week after she became the CEO of Axis.

She squinted at the unassuming little lines. *But the first payload was executed yesterday.*

This breach was happening right beneath her nose the entire time. She shuddered.

She recognized this type of backdoor– no, *spyware.* The billionaire willingly installed it onto his other systems before. This specific program was used by government investigators. Her deepest fear was confirmed. *How did I never notice it? How did they get away with it for so long?* She bit her nails. Had she adopted the same arrogance as the billionaire? Just sitting around all day drinking beer?

Have I become complacent?

At the end of the wall of code was plain text. A message.

Pick your loyalties, or we will pick them for you.

—

Josiah was waiting outside when she managed to stand back up and make her way to the door. She'd fallen to her knees in shock. Her legs were still shaking like jelly. His face, red-hot with resentment at first, softened with concern once he got a good look at her.

"Jesus," he said, "you look terrible."

"I *can't* get you roped into what I just found," Veronica interrupted. All of her words melted into each other. She couldn't help but slur her speech after such a large adrenaline rush. "I can't. Don't ask. I won't tell. And please, for the love of God, just fucking trust me on this." She clutched her cross pendant. "Please. You need to work with me on this. It's for your own peace of mind."

The corner of Josiah's mouth twitched. "That...is the opposite of conducive to my peace of mind."

"Well, then it's for your *protection*."

Josiah swallowed hard and nodded in response. He was staring at her like she had two heads.

They walked together. Veronica looked down at her shoes. It was an odd sight to behold, especially for any employee that happened to pass her– to see a woman who was typically so composed carry herself with so much resignation.

Josiah broke the silence first. "I'm sorry for...implying the things I implied," he said.

Veronica picked her head up in surprise. She looked at him with a trace of disbelief, but when she saw only sincerity in his expression, she let her guard back down.

"Yeah," she muttered. "Me too."

They were quiet for a while longer. Just as Veronica was about to enter her office, she heard a familiar voice carry through the hallway. She and Josiah exchanged another look. They both recognized it at the same time.

"No...it's like, not like that," Nancy called clearly.

"Then what's it like?"

"Not like *that*. I can't tell you specifically..."

"C'mon. Why not?" The other voice teased. There was a hint

of bitterness in its tone. Veronica was reminded of the way a mean high school girl speaks to quiet students.

"She told me not to."

"*She told you not to?* Nancy, what's going on in that office?"

"Nothiiing!" She drew out the last syllable like an embarrassed schoolgirl, a trace of a giggle in her voice. Veronica could almost *hear* her blushing.

Veronica frowned at Josiah. She gave him a look as if to say, *See? See how hard it is for Nancy to* not *make it sound like we have some weird gross office romance shit going on between us?*

Josiah pursed his lips. He could only offer her a sympathetic nod.

14

GROWN

Patterned strawberries lined the borrowed pair of pajamas Veronica wore. The pants' hem rested high above her ankle, but they sufficed just fine– after all, it was just meant to be sleep-wear, she reasoned. Daisy donned a cheeky nightgown. That, on the other hand, *really* would have been too short to be decent on Veronica. So strawberry pajamas it was.

Daisy sat on the floor with criss-crossed legs. Veronica looked right through her with sympathetic, burning eyes, taking in the full weight of just how oblivious Daisy was to all of the things happening to her little world. Pressure tightened her chest. Veronica really was that little world's sole guardian, and any mishandling of its contents was entirely her responsibility. But she was so helpless. So very helpless.

"Something's wrong," Daisy said. "I can tell."

Not as oblivious as she thought. It's not like she was too

stupid to read Veronica, after all. Her mouth twitched. "You're right," she responded, her cadence dry and defeated. She couldn't even try to deny it. There was no point. "I just...don't really know how to tell you about it. Or if I should? It's not anything that you can do anything about, anyway. Look..." she bit her lip and braced herself for the next part of her sentence. "There's kind of a chance that your world is being targeted? I shut down everything a–"

Though Daisy's face remained stiff, her eyes glossed over. A subtle change, considering the room's low lighting. "I don't want to know any more than that."

"*What?*"

"I don't want to know any more than that," Daisy repeated.

"Why?"

"Would you want to know if your world was potentially facing total destruction? If a fatal meteor was going to strike it during your lifetime? If a solar flare had a chance of wiping everyone on your planet out for good? No," she continued, "So I don't really want to know either." She looked down in her lap for a beat. When she looked at Veronica again, the gloss in her eyes had become borderline tears. "And to be honest, I wish you wouldn't talk to me about that stuff anymore, okay? I've had enough unbearable knowledge for one lifetime."

Veronica did not relate. *Yes,* she thought to herself. *I would want to know all of those things. I'd want to know absolutely every-thing.* But regardless of whether she personally understood or not, she still felt ashamed for hurting her. "I'm sorry," she whispered hoarsely. She *knew* she shouldn't have told Daisy anything.

And for what? Her own selfish need to vent? Veronica wished she'd been more considerate of what she'd been through.

Daisy smiled. "It's okay. It really is. Don't worry about it."

"I mean…" Veronica's face grew hot with embarrassment. She was so flustered, she couldn't bring herself to look at anything but her own knees. "Just. I'm going to protect this world with everything I have, no matter what. I promise."

It was quiet for a while.

Daisy broke the silence first. "You're so cool, you know," she said. Her voice carried a trace of playfulness. Veronica wasn't sure whether she was trying to distract Veronica or distract herself, but she appreciated the gesture either way.

"Cool? Really? How?" Veronica shot back. Her baffled tone was earnest. Daisy giggled.

"Look at you. You're so *melodramatic*." She heightened her voice a little bit to mimic Veronica's. "'I'm going to protect you with everything I have. No matter what.' You're intense. But you know what? You definitely know how to make it work."

"You *wish* I said that," she shot back. "I said I'll protect this *world*. I didn't say anything about you, specifically."

"You might as well have." Just like that, Daisy turned serious. Veronica felt bashful. She clutched one of Daisy's pillows and folded her legs into her chest.

"Well," she sputtered, "of course I want to protect you. You're my friend." She took a deep breath. "Out of fear of sounding *melodramatic*," she said, shooting Daisy another jovial glance, "you're one of the few people that understands me. In my world, I have to be on all the time. Constantly. I've been through a lot. *He's*…put me through a lot. *Still* puts me through a lot," she sneered. "Even post-mortem." As soon as the words left her mouth, she covered it up. "Uh. I'm sorry. You probably don't want to talk about–"

"No," Daisy said. "Please continue, it's fine. You sound like you need to talk about it...you know, with someone who *under-stands?*"

"You're giving me mixed signals. I thought you were tired of knowing about bad things?"

"Not bad things. *Existentially* bad things. Things that humans aren't equipped to handle. I mean, you and I both know that it's all too common in both of our worlds for abusers to royally fuck up people's wellbeing. And trust me, when it comes to *that* bastard, I am entirely prepared to handle whatever you have to share with me. It might be good for us."

Veronica bit her thumb. She slowly exhaled. "Okay," she said. "Are you sure it will be good for you?"

"Positive," Daisy replied. "Do you know how hard it is to talk about this shit with people from my *own* world? And more importantly, it'll be good for *you*, Ronnie. Let me hear it."

Ronnie, she thought. *She's never called me that before.* "Alright," she started. She cleared her throat and lay down on the couch, then shifted until she was comfortable. Just like she was in a therapy session. She half-expected Daisy to laugh while she pre-pared herself, but she didn't. Just stared at her with patient, knowing eyes.

"Um, let me give you some context. I was thirteen. I came from a pretty poor household. My mom died when I was just five...the works. She died accidentally. Just pure bad luck. So I moved in with my dad, who never *expected* to *actually* end up being a father...he's not a bad guy, you know, it's just...complicated?" She threw her arms above her head, a broad and vague gesture. Daisy said nothing. Just continued to attentively wait and listen. "Anyway," Veronica continued, feeling self-consciousness creep up on her, "I managed to get into this program at Yale for gifted teens in STEM when I was thirteen–"

"Hm...what's that?" Daisy questioned, her voice soft.

"Huh?"

"Yale?"

A trace of a smile danced on Veronica's lips. Daisy's way of asking questions about her world was always endearing. "Right. It's a university. Not to brag, but it's also one of the best that we have."

"Oh, I'm sure it is," Daisy teased. "Go ahead and fluff it up for the girl who doesn't know anything, am I right?"

"It really is!" she laughed. "*Anyway,* I was thirteen years old. The youngest to ever get into that program– *really*." She turned her head back toward Daisy and flashed her a smirk. Daisy smiled and looked at the floor. "He just so happened to get into the same program as me. He was seventeen at the time. We developed a rivalry of sorts. I mean, if you ask me, *he's* the one who started it. Not to sound full of myself, but I think that he was a little threatened by the fact that there was this thirteen-year-old girl who was constantly neck-to-neck with him. And..." she grimaced, a mixture of shame and disgust painting her expression. "I've never told anyone about this before, but I had this little schoolgirl crush on the guy. I can't imagine why anymore...Probably because I felt like I *had* to pick some guy to like, and he was the only one I knew. It didn't last for very long.

Because something weird happened. We grew closer, then we became friends. He became more like a mentor to me. What he didn't know about technology, he made up for with his knowledge of business. Or, you know what, I'll just come out and say it— it wasn't his knowledge of business, it was the fact that he was born into money. He wasn't always the most ethical. The dude was a nepo-baby raised by people who owned some of the biggest companies in the world. But shit, how was I supposed to know any better? I was a kid." She took a moment to pause and breathe. Still, Daisy said nothing, retaining her patient air.

"Well, we ended up planning out this whole company together. Axis. We'd be co-owners. We had it all figured out. I had the tech knowledge, he had the money and know-how to run the thing. But when it was almost time for us to actually graduate and get it started..." She exhaled sharply. "Things went to *shit.* It was my eighteenth birthday, I was already done with my master's...all but officially. He was a super senior. Partied too much, had to retake some classes. On Daddy's dime, of course, so it was all just fine and dandy. He organized the entire thing for me. A little too loud for my liking, a little too extravagant, but I thought to myself, *okay, that's just how he is. He's trying to be nice.* Do you know what he does?" At that point, she was shaking.

"The fucker tells me he's in love with me and *propositions me.* Said that he'd loved me for a very long time. That he wants to have sex with me. On my eighteenth birthday! He was twenty-two, and he'd known me since I was barely a teen. I mean, that's some iffy shit, right? I didn't even know how to respond. I got mad at him for putting the company at risk, first and foremost. Why let petty feelings get in the way of what we were building?

His expression just *dropped.* I couldn't even really get a read on him, it's like his emotions just fell off his face. I asked him if he thought of me that way when I was thirteen. You know what he says next?"

Daisy gently placed her hand over Veronica's. "Mhm?" she prompted.

"He says that I was *just so mature for my age.* And...and next thing you know, I'm not fucking building this company *with* him anymore, I'm basically demoted to head engineer. 'Conflict of interest', he says. What the fuck?" At that point, Veronica had started crying. She didn't even realize it until she felt the tears drop onto her thighs, which caused the thin strawberry-patterned fabric to stick to her skin. Her back hunched over the pillow she was hugging. "And he uses the tech that *I* developed as a springboard for all...of his...*bullshit.*"

Daisy put her hand on her shoulder. "It's okay. I understa-"

She was interrupted when Veronica pulled her in for a deep hug. Daisy hugged her back and let Veronica bury her face into her shoulder. Daisy's shirt muffled small, quiet sobs. "It's okay, Ronnie," she continued, stroking her back. "I get it. Take all the time you need. You're not the only one, trust me, I know."

—

Veronica gently carried the chip she'd copied Daisy's old file to in the palm of her hand. It felt lighter than the chip she'd extracted from Eclipta, as if the weight of what Daisy had experienced at the hands of the billionaire was actual. A more innocent woman's soul rested in her hands. Blissfully unaware of the world, just like how Daisy wished she could be. But they were not the same person anymore– the Daisy in her hands was a different person than the Daisy she'd just spoken with. She knew that there was no point in incubating a soul that would never replace the friend she'd made, never even come to fruition again. *You can't just back up someone's entire personhood,* she thought. That thought made her shudder with guilt.

She placed the chip on the floor of her room. She heard Bratty's meow echo across the halls and jumped. She was still getting used to the cat being around again. A new wave of shame hit her. Did Bratty feel abandoned for those few days she was stuck at her old apartment? It dissipated as soon as the cat rubbed against her ankle, purring.

"Hi, Kitty," she said, squatting down to pet her. She picked up the hammer she'd left on the floor. Then, without another thought, she smashed the chip into pieces.

15

HOME

Daisy never got over the anxiety that came with every new therapy session, but it was reduced a little more with each visit, at least. The appointments still felt somewhat fruitless. She knew that some of the more general life advice her therapist gave her was helpful, and she also knew that it made her grandmother happy to see her go to her appointments. Both the therapist and her grandmother even went so far as to insist that they'd seen some *improvement* in her. But it felt like her improvement wasn't actually authentic improvement at all. At least, not according to her grandmother's standards, and certainly not her therapist's. There was no way to explain that the so-called improvement they saw in her was from making friends with an ethereal fifth-dimensional goddess. Who is also a human, somehow. *It sounds so stupid when I put it that way. Not to mention that it'll sound like I'm mentally unstable.*

...Not that I'm mentally stable, anyway.

Regardless, she was tired of dodging exactly *why* she was so damn happy, so at peace out of nowhere, every time she talked to her therapist. It wasn't just the coping skills she'd learned. It was Veronica. Her therapist picked up on that too.

"So," she began as soon as Daisy settled onto her chair, "last time you were here, we were talking about how much better you're doing. And that's great, Daisy. We've made a lot of progress together. That said..." she trailed off and tapped her pencil against her clipboard, lowering her head. A coy smile blossomed across her face. "I don't think that I can take all of the credit. Every time I ask you about your relationships, you insist that there isn't anybody that important. I'll be frank here— I don't think that's entirely true, is it? Humans are social creatures, and it seems like you've found someone outside of those four walls that's helping you along. I don't want to seem like I'm calling you a liar, and this will be the last time I ask before I drop it. But really, Daisy...who is it?" She set her clipboard onto her lap and gave her a playfully expectant look.

"I...guess there's someone," she mumbled.

"Okay."

"I have this...friend. She just kind of randomly came into my life? I don't know how to explain it. But it feels like she's the only one in the world who really understands my situation."

"Oh, that's nice! You should feel proud. And you know, I'm positive that you'll find others who understand you that way, too."

Daisy stopped herself from frowning. *No. I won't.*

—

She gazed at her own reflection and felt a strange sense of thankfulness at the sight of her own face. After what the billionaire did to her, it was something she was always cognizant of. Just how good it is for someone to have their own body. Their own face. To not live inside of a corpse. And as she stared, she thought about the exchange she had with Veronica the night before.

It was difficult to imagine that the woman who cried in her arms last night was the same woman who kidnapped her with such calloused precision. That same feeling struck her after they'd gone clubbing together. How could such a serious, solemn, hyper-competent woman let herself so loose and dance the way that Veronica did? Where did all of that *emotion* come from? She was struck with bone-deep sonder. It was so easy, convenient at times even, to be solipsistic. People don't only forget that others live lives just as complex as their own— sometimes, people intentionally put the thought out of their mind. *And not just people like the billionaire,* Daisy thought. *Not just people who are manipulative and self-centered.* If everyone was always aware of the deep complexity everyone around them held, it might drive everyone on the planet mad. She turned her head side-to-side, twisted her body, taking in the full breadth of her own physicality. If she was someone else and she saw herself walking down the street, what would she think? Would she even pay any mind to herself at all?

What did Veronica think of her?

As an object, upon their first meeting. An extension of the billionaire himself. Another one of his stupid, over-the-top tech projects. In her defense, she was sort of correct in that assessment, as self-deprecating as it felt to think of herself that way. It was a much more complicated situation than Veronica might have thought, though. What she'd done to Daisy in the past was long since made up for in the way she treated her in the present. Veronica validated things about her that nobody else would ever be able to, understood her and treated her in a way that nobody else ever could. From something as concrete as having similar bad experiences with the same shitty guy to something as unreal as being the only two people who possessed the knowledge they had regarding one another's worlds.

After Veronica spilled everything to Daisy and cried into her chest like they were lifelong friends, she became apologetic.

"I'm sorry," she'd said, wiping the tears away from her face with vigor. "I know that...isn't all as bad as what *you* went through with him. What you went through with *me*. And now I'm making you comfort me. I'm not usually like this, I promise."

But comforting her was so cathartic. "Don't apologize," Daisy whispered, brushing her fingers against Veronica's shoulder. "I should be thanking you."

Daisy once read somewhere that over time, the cells in one's retinas degrade and age, causing the colors a person sees to become less saturated the older they get. But her entire world looked more vibrant than ever before. The bright colors inside the club were fun when they were seen through intoxicated, dilated eyes– but she had now managed to find an even longer lasting satisfaction in the mundane. She didn't need to seek constant stimulation to run away from her reality. Maybe, just maybe, her reality was worth slowing down for.

She took off her shirt and peered at her naked torso. She

made herself aware of the weight of her breasts resting against the top of her stomach. Her skin was warm, orangish, soft and spilling over her waistband. Its slight furriness made it feel like flour-dusted dough to the touch. She'd usually be self-conscious of the fact that her chest was flatter than her stomach, that the button on her jeans wasn't visible, that her nipples pointed downward (*6:30 titties*, as the girls who happened to see her in the locker room would put it so derisively)...but in the moment, she was happy that her own body was hers. She saw no healed stab wound on her chest.

Despite all that she'd been through, all of the knowledge she was not meant to comprehend and was made to bear anyway, she was happier than she'd ever felt before. She had a friend.

—

The lights flickered on in the little house. It didn't feel lived in at all these days. It didn't even feel like *his space*, really. It was just where he and his kids slept. Josiah's tired eyes soaked in the aura surrounding him– cold, dull lighting erupted from a too-bright overhead fluorescent light. Different desaturated shades had been swatched with haphazard abandon onto the bare white walls around him. The only things that added any variety to the plain space. He meant to pick one of the colors and finish painting them at some point, but he was always too exhausted. And his exhaustion was constant. The raise and promotion he'd received when Veronica became the CEO of the company was nice, sure, and he easily could have upgraded his family's house given the size of his checks. Pay his ex-wife's rent on top of that. Hire an interior designer. Hire a maid, even. But those fantasies were all overwritten by his constant fretting about being too absent of a father. Life wasn't too bad, and he knew that– he could easily afford all of the kids' extracurriculars, quality dinners, cooking classes for himself too, counseling for his daughter, her new clothes, new makeup, medicine, new everything. The kids never had to want for anything. With the savings he had, they'd never have to worry about taking care of him either, decades down the line. Yet he still felt guilty. If he hired someone to clean up around the house, they might end up seeing the maid more than they saw *him.* How would it come across to his kids if he had to hire somebody else to do the cooking, cleaning, hell, even the *decorating?* He yearned for a space that didn't feel so damn empty. It would almost make him *happy* to come home to a mess, for once. It'd mean that they were expressing *some* kind of joy.

But they never did. They all sat in their rooms like they were toys in a long-abandoned dollhouse. They likely didn't even hear him come through the door. He kicked off his shoes and sighed as he lay down on the couch, office-like in its lack of usage and strange professional air. He thought that he and his ex-wife managed to set a decent example for his kids. He thought they were an excellent demonstration for how sometimes, relationships don't work out– and people can be *happy* that way. Regardless, the kids were taking it hard. He should have realized sooner that no matter how close he and his ex still were, regardless of the fact that they were still good friends, a big change like that was going to alter their lives forever no matter how they approached it. Their family was not the same anymore. It didn't feel like his kids needed their own father, and that worried him.

That line of thought crossed his mind all too often. Almost

every time he had the kids and almost every time he came home from work. Picking up his kids from his ex's house only made him jealous. Jealous of all of the drawings, all the toys strewn about, all the shrieking and playing. They just didn't act like that with him. His house was...well, just *Dad's house.* He burned with even more intense jealousy when she'd shrug and give him a crooked smile, tell him that she loved those kids, but God did they *wear her out* with their insistence on following her around, nagging, and "trying to crawl up her ass", as she put it. "Especially Lynn," she would say. "You'd think a teenager wouldn't be so needy."

Every time she said that, he wished so much harder that they'd all act that way with him as well.

"Dad?"

Josiah just about leapt out of his skin. *Speak of the devil.* "Lynn," he breathed, grasping his chest. "You scared the *shit* out of me."

His daughter's hands were folded behind her back. Her expression was too pleasant. Like she was face-to-face with someone she hardly knew. "Uh...sorry. Did you remember I have my class tonight?"

"Which one?" he responded, rubbing his eyes. *So many activities to keep up with.*

"Voice therapy," she reminded him. Her voice was soft and patient. "At the Pride Center."

"Right." A pang of fear hit him in the chest. It was complemented with a brand-new wave of guilt. He was nothing but supportive of Lynn, but he still could not help but feel the full gravity of how difficult the rest of her life would be for her. She'd already moved schools about three times due to the constant bullying. At the same time, he was ridden with a different kind of guilt– guilt that he felt anything other than pride that his daughter had found herself, pinpointed what was making her so angsty, and took the steps needed to find her own way to happiness. But even more so than those endless layers of shame, he was angry that nothing had changed. The world refused to make itself a safer place for his child.

...Am I making her issues about me?

And that only added yet another layer.

"I'm going to walk you inside," he added. "Just in case."

His daughter's face screwed up a little, but she said nothing.

The drive there was silent, and the drive back was even quieter.

—

"I'm telling you that it's really not...well, like *that,*" Nancy said, giggling into the microphone. "It's, like, I think that she likes me...no, it's not quid pro quo! Stop!" she erupted into laughter. She rolled onto her back and kicked her legs in the air, the soft mattress underneath her shifting with her weight. "It's so innocent. Really. Like, she took me out to lunch, asked me about my life, she was so respectful...like, she's one of the most powerful people in L.A. What is she supposed to do? Just not date anyone because there's a 'power imbalance?' Get real...No, I really don't think I'm going to regret it." Her voice turned serious. She got up and walked to her kitchenette– a very short walk, really, considering the size of her living space. She turned the dial on her brewer. It murmured as it boiled the water inside.

"Look, I'll say something to her if she doesn't say anything to me in like...the next few months."

"Didn't you say that she threatened to fire you just the other day?" the voice on the other line crackled. It was growing more incredulous by the minute. It was her sister. The only person in her family she could talk to about those things. It frustrated Nancy that she couldn't even talk about her love life judgment-free with the one person who she thought would understand. She vented that frustration by popping open her ramen cup with a flourish.

"Well, yeah," Nancy responded, more than a little impatient. "But she was just frustrated. She could've said that to anyone. It was a wrong place, wrong time kind of thing. I'm telling you, I think she likes me."

"And I think you might be misreading the situation. Because, like, it would be really inappropriate of her. And since when do you like girls?"

Nancy frowned. "Since now. Are you trying to say there's something wrong with that?"

"Girl, *no*. You act like we're still living in the 2010s. Nobody cares about *that*. I'm just worried that you're in love with the *attention*. Not with your boss. That's like, rule number one of being alive? Hello? Don't fuck your boss?"

"I am *not* fucking my boss, don't be gross," Nancy shot back.

"So why did she get so angry at you? Did you like, sneak into her office to come on to her?"

"No!" she shouted. "I'm tired of hearing people say that. Listen," she continued, lowering her tone. "...I'll tell you why she got so mad. But you cannot tell *anyone*. You understand?"

—

She lay on her cot in silence, her hands folded over her chest.

All of her furniture was moved into the room at last, which made its hospital-like air more reminiscent of hospice care. She stared up at the ceiling. The darkness ate its way through her eyes, causing them to produce small flashes of color and patterns. Maybe it was the smell that always managed to remind her of some kind of medical setting. Or the sound. That never-ending whirring and pumping of machines. The only thing that interrupted it and kept her from going insane right then and there was Bratty's soft little footsteps echoing off the hard, smooth walls.

Or maybe it was the way life-or-death situations always managed to find her, always managed to linger around her like a chronic sickness.

The door was locked. The pieces of chip she'd smashed earlier were tucked away in her drawer, also locked. And her eyes were still wide open.

Pick my loyalties for me. Force me to work with the R.O.C. or the U.S.A.? Give up Project Metaworld? Kill everyone in it? Pick my loyalties for me... she clutched her comforter. *You can assign whatever loyalties you want to someone after they're dead. They'll tell the world I was a dirty communist. Crooked. A predator, probably...a traitor. A killer. The billionaire's killer.*

She was not going to get much sleep that night. She would not be getting much sleep for a very long time.

PART TWO

16

BREAK

Veronica was not yet awake when she stumbled her way out of bed. Bratty's demanding meows beat her alarm clock to the punch– first invading her dreams, then forcing her to get up. Her joints clicked as her feet kicked away the warm covers and hit the freezing floor. Back to cold, uncaring reality. She felt weightless at first, even peaceful, but it did not last; the real world sunk back into her bones and settled beneath her skin. With incredible difficulty, she kept her eyes somewhat open as she popped open a can of food for the cat. Then she brewed a pot of coffee.

What's it going to be today? she thought, staring at the golden-brown stream splashing against the bottom of her mug. It made her train of thought steer toward a longing for waterfalls and nature walks and warm baths, all of which she could not indulge in. *And how am I going to prepare myself to handle it?*

She was not supposed to be awoken by her alarm clock for another thirty minutes. That made plenty of time to sit and think, since she knew she wouldn't be able to fall asleep again. Even if she tried, it would be a dangerous game to play. She'd only gotten about two hours of real shut-eye. There was a serious risk that she would sleep through her alarm *and* Bratty's crying if she went back to bed.

She showered, brushed her teeth, threw on some clothes that made her look presentable and respectable *enough*– nothing that would cause her outfit to end up in a trashy tabloid. "CEO Fashion Blunder", the title might have read. It was not lost on her how strange it was that she had to take that into consideration at all. She couldn't pull off the "Super-intelligent CEO who doesn't care about their appearance as much as the work they do" look that so many others managed. *Just don't fit the demographic*, she thought, rubbing moisturizer into her cheeks with contemptuous vigor. *Always going to be defined by my appearance.*

The way that the general public perceived her clothing choices was, of course, not the root of her grumpiness that day. But it was the easiest thing for her to focus on. Everything else was too far out of the bounds of her control.

She triple-checked that she locked the door behind her before she headed to her office, but she still felt uneasy. She wondered if any attempts at security were even worth anything at all anymore.

The building was quiet. On a typical day, she'd like being the only person strolling through the halls, the click of her heels against smooth floors satisfyingly cracking through the silence...but it felt strange that time. As if she was not actually the only person there. Would she ever feel alone again? Nothing seemed like it was worth anything at all anymore. Was she really that powerless when it came down to it?

Could she reclaim what little power she had over her life if she gave the government what they wanted? Stepped down from the company, or gave them access to all of her tech...

...Or allowed them to use her proprietary technology to develop extreme weaponry?

She sneered at the mere thought. Resentment bubbled in her, but it fizzled out when another wave of powerlessness crashed through her chest.

I just need to lay low. Or figure out a way to get one over on–
No. You're not going to get one over on the government.
It won't happen. It's not possible. You can't possibly be that obtuse.
She felt like crying.

—

Veronica stared at the entrance to her office from her desk, half-lidded, head animalistic in its emptiness. She'd been like that for about twenty minutes by then. She had a vague awareness of the passage of time, of the fact that she wasn't doing anything productive in particular, but she couldn't bring herself to do anything else. It might have been out of fear of finding something new that would disturb her, threaten her, or otherwise make her feel unsafe. She'd almost rather if she were in the position she was in before. It was easier to be a whistleblower, to remain invisible and still have access to all of the billionaire's secrets as she liked. The one who made sure he never gained too much of an advantage over the rest of the world. Kept him human.

But did she really succeed? Was it ever possible to succeed? She thought she was in the best possible position to prevent the atrocities he committed from ever happening again, but really, she was either going to be forced into the role that the billionaire filled for the government or she would be assassinated. Perhaps that's why he chose to leave the company to her all along. Was he even capable of thinking things through like that? Then again, he *could* be quite the conniving bastard. He must have known she would be incapable of taking on his position, not out of a lack of skill, but a lack of support. The general population hated her down to the core of who she was. The government found her threatening. Perhaps he just wanted her to be beaten into submission, whether he was there to witness it or not. He always knew that she took issue with his lack of ethics. He always knew that she struggled to connect with her coworkers, who had then become her resentful employees, because of her refusal to concede to the governments' fascist ideology.

That *prick*.

She couldn't let it happen

She pivoted toward her window. It was full-length from floor to ceiling. She'd covered it up with a blackout curtain a few hours prior. She peeked through it. There was a long line of vehicles streaming into Axis HQ's parking garage. People of all ages walked toward the entrance in a line moving opposite of the traffic, dressed up in drab, corporate colors. She only recognized some of them. She heard some voices outside of her office, the sound of footsteps, even laughter. Most were headed toward one of the many cafés and kitchenettes around the campus. Her stomach growled. She *was* hungry. Maybe she could stand to grab a bite to eat, she thought.

But the laughter and conversation came to a screeching halt as soon as she walked out of her office. She was used to people fearing her a little, sure– after all, she was the *big boss*. But not quite to this extent. *Maybe I look a little rougher than usual...a little meaner? It's not like this has been the* best *morning of my life. Far from it.* She used her phone as a mirror. Her eye bags were a little darker, she supposed. The beginning of crow's feet around her eyes just a tad bit deeper than usual. Nothing *too* out of the ordinary, nothing to warrant that jarring of a response.

It dawned on her that her sleep deprivation could have been contributing to how she was interpreting their behavior.

And my hunger. Did I even eat last night? She rubbed her eyes, trying to regain her focus. *Right. Headed to a kitchenette...I'll get myself a bowl of cereal.*

She ignored the eerie silence from the people filling the hall around her and straightened her back, trying and failing to spark an air of authority to her as if she were flicking an empty lighter.

She hadn't been to an Axis kitchenette in a very long time. It was less drab and empty than it was before she became the CEO, she supposed. She could enjoy the small amount of satisfaction that came from that, at least. That change was due to one of her controversial decisions as CEO that she never actually *expected* to be controversial. Before then, there were only a couple kitchenettes in the entire building and they were never stocked. The employees usually brought their own supplies or snacks, and they were sometimes kind enough to share them with others. That often looked like a team leader bringing donuts on tough days to boost morale, keeping granola bars around, something like that. There were a few vending machines around, too. But that was it. The mini-city corporate campuses that were so popular in the 20s had long since fallen out of vogue, and the billionaire was never shy about voicing how much he was against the idea. He thought that it infantilized employees. "My company's headquarters are not Disneyland. We come here to work." That quote became popular and started making its rounds just as soon as it came out of his mouth. Low-level leaders of all shapes and sizes fell in love with using it to justify their own shittiness.

She frowned and turned the knob on one of the many dispensers lined up on the kitchenette's counters. A generous heap of cereal poured into a little plastic bowl. She had no clue just how beloved that quote was until after she'd decided to rework HQ's facilities. She set up construction on a few cafés and a centralized cafeteria, then she ordered that staff be hired to restock self-service stations in kitchenettes that contained juice machines, waffle makers, cereal dispensers, the like. Possibly it became a popular quote after the work had already started, and perhaps her decision was so controversial for the mere fact that it contradicted her predecessor's vision. Conspiracy theorists had a field day with every little thing she did that could be interpreted as a sleight against the billionaire— which felt like just about every decision she made, really.

And maybe government officials would, too.

She shuddered at the reminder. *Have they found anything related to my work against the billionaire? What would they do with that? What's going to become of me?*

A crisp snapping sound sent her back to reality. She'd pressed her plastic spoon so hard against the bottom of her bowl, it broke in half. She blinked and rubbed her eyes, then stood up to get another one. Her face felt hot. She hoped that nobody saw what happened.

As she leaned against the counter, fishing through a basket full of plastic-wrapped cutlery, she picked up on a voice in her proximity. It spoke in a hushed whisper, which only made the contents of what it was saying more alluring. She held her breath and strained her ears to listen.

"...There was a data breach. They didn't tell us, but there *was* one."

Veronica's breath caught in her throat.

"Really? What did they find?"

"We don't know. *Nobody* knows."

"Who did it?"

"That's the thing. All I've heard is that it couldn't have been one of us...it was completed remotely, from outside of the building. What if it was..."

She could no longer hold herself back. Veronica turned around and placed her hand on one of the speaker's shoulders. A bespectacled middle-aged man. She didn't recognize him, and she didn't think that she was the one who hired him. Their first interaction, maybe. "I think that's enough of that conversation," she muttered. Her voice was hoarse and intense.

Every part of his face widened. His eyes popped open and his jaw dropped. He didn't say a single word. Was that a tad of resentment she caught in his expression? A little bit of suspicion? A questioning of her authority?

She refused to break her gaze. A reflection of her tired, angry expression stared back at her through his glasses. Even through that translucent and distorted image of herself, she could tell that her eyes were bloodshot. She looked frightening, and she did not care.

"It's been taken care of," she continued. "I don't tolerate unproductive and petty *gossip* at Axis." She shot a look at his conversation partner, a woman of about the same age. She was as pale as a sheet. After a few seconds of that tension, she realized that the entire room was silent.

All eyes were on her, judging her.

Staring right through me. Hating me.

"Do something better with your time," she announced, then stalked back out of the room, leaving her meal behind. She did not hear any conversation start back up the entire way back to her office.

—

She stayed cooped up behind her computer for the rest of that work day. Responded to emails, checked on the status of a few odd projects, and drank more than a few beers. After that, she deteriorated into writing, then scribbling, in her notebook. She would have typed on her computer, but she no longer trusted it. Every camera in her office had been disconnected and taped over. She tore every microphone out of every device in the room. Had her phone on airplane mode for the day. Topics she vented about included her general frustration, her past with the billionaire, about just how scared she was. How she still felt like a little girl deep inside.

How she didn't know how she got wrapped up in any of this. How she didn't understand why people were so damn proud of her. She hadn't done a single thing to be proud of. She wasn't even thirty yet, and this is where her life had taken her. It wasn't fair.

The notebook's pages were wrinkled and smudged with tears by the time the sienna late-afternoon sun dappled on the floor from in between her curtains. She looked outside just as she had that morning. It looked the same as the scene from earlier, only reversed– cars leaving the parking garage, people walking in the opposite direction like they were on a factory line. How did they let themselves become so *mechanical?* So routine-oriented?

How did she let herself become that way, too?

When the California sun melted into the skyscrapers in the distance, turning the afternoon into evening, she checked the cameras around the building one last time. Nobody was there, from what she could see. The janitors long since went home. *It's Friday,* she remembered. That meant she would be left alone over the weekend. Well, for the most part. She could still shut down the building altogether and refuse to let anyone in at all, even the overachievers who liked to come to the office and complete their work over the weekend.

Good. That was exactly what she was going to do.

About an hour and a couple more beers after that, she locked down the entire building and left the room. And ever so meticulously, she searched through every single corner of Axis Headquarters. She acted as if she were in a trance, digging through places as innocuous as an intern's junk drawer and as protected as rooms full of logs that detailed the creation of some of the most important technology of their era. She carried armfuls of paper, hard drives, folders, entire computers into what used to be Daisy's room– the only empty room at Axis HQ she could remember off the top of her head. She separated the data she did not recognize but still seemed important, mostly found in the billionaire's personal stash, from the endless amount of tech housing all of the secrets she was already privy to. It was sparse, which meant she could fit all of it in the safe inside of her living quarters. She decided that she would examine all of it on a different day.

With persistence, Daisy's old room was soon filled with every piece of sensitive data she could find. Veronica bit her lip. It was almost stacked to the ceiling, reminiscent of a hoarder house. So much and so little all at the same time. How awe-striking it was that every bit of sensitive information everyone at Axis ever produced was right there in front of her. Tangible.

And able to be destroyed.

She gripped a hammer in her hand. With a heavy grunt, she slung it behind her shoulder, then brought it down onto a computer with a scream. It lodged itself inside of the plastic casing. She ripped it out with some difficulty, then threw it back down. Again. And again. And again.

When she was satisfied with that one, she moved on to the next. Wash, rinse, repeat. She tore folders, brought a lighter to papers, snapped discs in half, and stomped on hard drives. She continued for hours without stopping a single time, her banshee-esque screams growing more frantic by the second. About half-way through her rampage, she dropped the hammer and started punching the machinery. The feeling of blood dripping down her knuckles joined the tears falling down her cheeks, sliding off of her and mixing into a sick pink combination on the bare floor. The skin on her knee ripped open when she put it through a laptop's screen. She paid it no mind. She worked until there was nothing of substance left in that room or in her. It was like a spell was broken when she was finished with her destruction. She became weak and fell onto her raw knees. She gripped her hair. She sobbed, then screamed, then howled. *I just want to go home. I just want to go home.*

I want my mother.

—

By the time Veronica calmed down enough to face anything other than her own bedroom, the sun was trudging itself back over the Los Angeles skyline. Orange light streamed through the rows of windows in the hallway. She squinted as she walked out and locked the door behind her. The light poured into her sensitive pupils, dilated from the darkness. She pressed her palms into her eye sockets. *I'm never going to be comfortable again, am I?* she thought, feeling more miserable than ever.

She limped back out of the wing and locked its entrance, as well. She'd already taken a shower, bandaged herself up, and changed her clothes. She didn't make any contact with Daisy at all– Veronica was far too ashamed of how pathetic she must have looked. As she walked toward her office, she tried to decide on what she'd say if anyone asked her what happened to her over the weekend. Biking accident? A bad fall down the stairs? She hoped nobody would notice at all. She couldn't afford to show any signs of weakness. *Everything's normal,* she thought. *I'm going to act like everything's normal.*

She walked inside of her office and slid behind her desk. But before she could finish lowering herself into her chair, a sharp gasp erupted from her lips.

An envelope was taped to her computer monitor. It was addressed to her.

Her breaths came out in gasps. She peeled it off the screen, fumbling it in her attempts to rip it open. She held the typed letter underneath her desk, trying hard to focus on the words through her vision-blurring anxiety.

Veronica,

You're beginning to run out of options. We are willing to work with you, but you have demonstrated no interest in working with us. There is a point when we must assume that it is because you have allegiances outside of serving the countries that have helped you work your way up from your impoverished childhood into the position of power you hold now.

Or perhaps you have gained your power through scientific means that neither the R.O.C. or the U.S.A. would approve of.

Your consistent and flagrant disrespect of the man who held this role before you is not something that the general public approves of. A woman in your position would surely understand how simple it would be to chalk his disappearance up to foul play. Who do you believe the most likely perpetrator of that foul play would be?

You are going to kill innocent civilians in your refusal to provide the information that we need. Even your employees have made you aware of this fact. Yet you still refuse. Perhaps part of the reason why is because you are too preoccupied with pretend play and petty escapism. That is something that we could easily remove you from.

We are still leaving the door open. If you do not reach out to us in a timely manner, we will assume that you are a threat to the state, and you should expect that your company will soon be under new management.

Kindest regards.

17

CATALYST

Probably they already knew about the safe she kept in her living area, she reasoned. Having a safe there was too obvious, anyway. She couldn't believe her own carelessness– she might as well have painted it neon yellow, slapped a target on it, and *invited* them to find a way to break into it. *That is, if they haven't figured out the combination to it already.*

Those thoughts rushed through her mind, matching her pace as she sprinted back toward her bedroom. *How did they get into the building? How did they get inside my office? Oh God, they're probably able to get into my bedroom, too...did they hear my screams? Is my cat okay?*

She thrust open her door.

Everything was exactly as she left it. Bratty's meow was as sweet and oblivious as ever to the fear and exhaustion emanating off Veronica. She wanted to stop, scoop her up, and hold her in her arms, feel thankful that it *at least* didn't seem that they touched anything inside of her room, but she had no time. She jiggled the lock on the safe with fervor after she entered the combination. It broke open. Such a trivial attempt at security, she realized. Such a method was reduced to utter child's play, given the circumstances. She swept everything inside of it onto the floor. The only things that seemed like they were worth investigating, that were so secured when she found them that they *had* to have sensitive information inside, were two manila folders and a hard drive. Her shaky hands made the folder flutter as she opened it. Her fingers flicked through the pages. Something related to Project Darwin. Nothing of importance about it. Nothing that she didn't know already. Why would the billionaire print this off? She threw it to the side. *I've looked at it, now I can destroy it. Safe inside my head. I'm the only person who needs to know.* Her own frenzy only disturbed her more.

The second folder. Only one paper lay inside. *Strange...*

She flipped it open. Whatever it was, it was written in code. It was all numeric, printed off in Calibri on a shabby piece of everyday printer paper. It looked amateurish and unassuming. Yet she did not recognize the code, and there were no tells that could point her toward any specific encryption method.

Okay, she thought, her hands shaking, *I have tools for this. I can figure this out. I mean, he was the one who encrypted this. How hard could it be?*

She booted up a private system she'd transferred to her new room a while ago. It was where she kept her decryption software. She knew that all of the units in her room were as secure as she could make them, but that did not quell her anxiety. She could not allow a single soul to get a hold of that information, whatever it was. *So much pressure.*

As it loaded, she thought more about what kind of encryption method might have been used. She squinted at the paper and tilted her head. *As if that'll help me figure it out.* She bit her thumb. *It was produced before he left for the island, at the absolute latest...so about a year ago.* She scratched her head and tried to recall where she found the folder.

In his old office. The one he used before he moved somewhere bigger. That would've been approximately three years ago.

So three years ago, at the latest. What method was most popular with the company at that time? Would he have even used the same encryption methods as his employees?

She unlocked her phone. It was still in airplane mode. Not that it had any service anyway, due to the thick metal walls of her living quarters. She opened her email app and scoured through it.

encryption before:01/01/2063

"Please let me find something," she whispered.

About 40 or so emails popped up. Most were from her own employees asking questions meant for the cybersecurity team. Rather than forwarding them, Veronica tended to respond to them herself, so her inbox at the time was bloated with them. There was one old email from the billionaire.

Staff training: encryption methods, the subject line read.

She tapped it so hard she almost dropped her phone.

But nothing inside of it gave her any information.

She groaned.

Is it even an encrypted message? What if it's just taken out of context?

...Then why is it the only paper in this folder? Why was it handled so carefully that I didn't even find it until I went looking for it? Why did he keep it around in his old office? All alone, hidden behind so many layers of security?

She stared at the paper again. That time, she took extra care to take in every single number on it.

30.97474.92232.060:72.63020.18028.08532.060

Nothing.

Veronica skipped over it for then. Maybe there would be something more helpful to her inside of the hard drive, if she was lucky. She inserted it in her laptop and prayed that it would not be something malicious. It very well could have been programmed to format itself if it was inserted in anything other than a specific machine.

Nothing of the sort happened. Instead, a password entry screen appeared— not dissimilar to the one that was used for Project Metaworld. How strange. If she were him, she would not have allowed something that was so sensitive to be loaded on just anyone's computer. Then again, the billionaire never was too meticulous with his security. Which only made Veronica feel even crazier about the fact that she could not figure out what those numbers *meant.*

ONE ATTEMPT LEFT, the screen read ominously. There was only an eight-letter long character limit. The numbers on the paper could not have been the password, itself: not that the billionaire would have been quite *that* idiotic, she reasoned. Those three words seemed to be challenging her. Go ahead. See what happens. It could range from something as small as the hard drive erasing its own data to something as big as what happened on the island.

She was so frustrated, she wanted to cry. There was only one chance to figure out the password, she couldn't figure out something that the *billionaire* had ciphered for God's sake, the government was after her, and worst of all, she no longer had any information to give them even if she *wanted* to. She was half-thankful that it was all destroyed before they could take it through brute force, half-terrified that her only way out no longer existed.

You can't just get one over on the government, she remembered.

Did she have any other option by then? Did she *ever* have any other option?

If I'm going to die, she thought, *I'm going to die with nothing for those bastards to rob me of.*

She gnawed on her lip, which was already raw and bloody.

Veronica could only think of one person she could still turn to for help.

—

"Where have you *been?*" Daisy asked, whisper-shouting. They were standing on the sidewalk by the park across from Daisy's apartment. Her grandmother was home, so Veronica waited by their window until she noticed her. Though Daisy's reaction to someone waiting outside of her window for her was less intense than Veronica anticipated it would be, it was still not the most ideal response either way. "You haven't been around for days, then you just decide to turn up at the worst time? It's the weekend. My grandma isn't going anywhere today."

"I know." Veronica's voice was flat and feverish.

"So what's going on? There has to be something going on." Her eyes were wide and pleading. A couple of heartbeats passed, accentuated by the distant sound of a bird chirping. It'd be peaceful in any other situation. Daisy opened her mouth as if she were going to add something else. She sighed and closed it, opting to keep staring expectantly at Veronica instead.

"...You kind of asked me not to tell you about it."

The corner of Daisy's mouth quirked. She was annoyed that Veronica had a point. She let out another, deeper sigh. "Okay then. Can't you just leave those parts out?"

"I mean, I can try?"

"Please do." Daisy squatted down and sat on the curb. Veronica joined her. "You know," she added, "I...want you to feel comfortable talking to me about stuff that's stressing you out, it's just..." she paused. "Hard when it has to do with the status of the entire world I live in. I had it taken from me before, and–"

She stopped her. "I know. And I'm not going to let it happen again. But I need you to *help* me not let it happen again."

Daisy's eyes darted back toward Veronica. They held newfound curiosity.

"I need you to help me decipher something. You're the only person who can help me out of here...Daisy, the government is after me." Her eyes welled up with tears. "I don't even know *which* government. Both, probably? Not that it matters. I need you to help me protect you. To help me protect *me*."

"You would know more about it than I do." Daisy's tone was uneasy and awe-struck. "What do you need me for? I can't do anything for you, I'm just...a mentally ill deli worker." She laughed without humor. "You *have* to know that I can't help you with something like this."

"You're the only person I can talk to right now," she replied. Her voice cracked on the word *talk*. "*Please.* I don't have time."

Daisy placed her head between her legs and pinched the bridge of her nose. After a few moments passed by, she flung her body upright as if she was shrugging off her anxiety. "Okay," she said. "Since you're out of options, let's take a look. I'll do my best. No promises, though."

They gazed at the code together, and more silence passed by. *How peaceful,* Veronica thought. Mourning doves called out to potential lovers, the lazy sun crawled up the sky...then she noticed that bird calls in Daisy's universe were different from the bird calls in her own. Still recognizable, though– had she not been paying attention, she wouldn't have noticed. It was a nice little escape from the daunting task at hand. Minutes passed before Daisy looked back up at the sheet.

She clicked her tongue. "I don't–" She stopped. "...Wait."

A heartbeat passed after she interrupted herself. She pulled the sheet closer to her face.

"What?" Veronica prodded.

"These decimals have a pattern. Five numbers between each decimal, except at the beginning and the..." she trailed off and squinted harder. "Hang on," she muttered. "Two numbers at the start before the first decimal, three at the end after the last decimal, still five...Okay. I think I have a pen." She produced one from her pocket and scribbled underneath the string of numbers.

$$30.97474.92232.060:72.63020.18028.08532.060$$
$$30.974\ 74.922\ 32.060:\ 72.630\ 20.180\ 28.085\ 32.060$$

"The way the first and last decimals are separated tells me that *this* should be the right pattern. And 32.060 shows up *twice*."

"That probably means that each number corresponds with a specific written symbol, probably a letter," Veronica said excitedly. "Maybe 32.060 even corresponds with a specific punctuation mark? Which means this cipher is a lot simpler than I thought. I just need to figure out what each number corresponds with."

"Wouldn't it be a pretty short message if each number only corresponded with *one* letter?" Daisy questioned. "It probably corresponds with a group of letters. Or maybe a word?"

"The first is probably more likely. I don't see why an entire word would be used twice."

"I mean, it's possible."

"Let's consider our more likely option first. There's more you can do with a group of letters rather than an entire word, and I don't think he was smart enough to come up with an entire dictionary of words that correspond with numbers."

Daisy raised an eyebrow at Veronica. "Or letter groups, for that matter. It probably corresponds with a key that he *didn't* make up. Something more commonly known?"

She's become pretty self-assured for someone who was just reducing herself to a "mentally ill deli worker," Veronica thought, amused.

She nodded in agreement. "That...was certainly his way of

doing things," she said. Veronica sucked air through her teeth. "...I really hope that's how he did it this time, too. What's the relevance of these decimals?"

Their attention turned back to the paper. Veronica couldn't help but feel more than a little embarrassed. If her mind weren't running at a million miles a minute, she definitely would have been competent enough to deduce what Daisy came up with. *Of course. Two before the first decimal, three after the last, of course that should've told me how those numbers were meant to be separated.* She rubbed her temples and sighed. She would never say so out loud, but she hadn't considered just how clever Daisy is in quite a while. She had to escape from the billionaire *somehow,* after all, not that the billionaire is all that smart in the first place— but that would've taken a lot of problem-solving on Daisy's part anyway, wouldn't it? Guilt settled in her stomach. Why had it been so long since Veronica recognized her intelligence? Did that make her just as bad as everyone else in the hardened, sick world that dehumanized the Alien Girl to such great extents?

As if answering her thought, Daisy snapped her fingers. "The atomic mass of Neon is 20.180. Right there. 20.180. The groups of letters must correspond with the periodic table."

Veronica's eyes grew to the size of saucers. "...That was quick," was all she could offer. Daisy laughed.

"Do I not seem smart? Be honest."

"No, no, it's not that, I didn't think you were *stupid,* for sure—"

"It's okay. I know I'm not that smart," Daisy interrupted. "Really. I'm just...good at reciting random facts."

She smiled. "Don't say that. I *do* think you're smart."

Her eyes lingered on Veronica, surprised. Then her face broke into a big grin. "Let's get this figured out," she finished, turning her bashful expression away from her.

—

Phosphorous Arsenic Sulfur : Germanium Neon Silicon Sulfur

PAsS: GeNeSiS

She chewed on her fingernail and typed the password into her laptop. Her fingertips lingered on each individual key long after she'd pressed it. Just in case it was case sensitive, she entered it exactly as it appeared with no correction. She must have double-checked it about seven times before she decided to hit the enter key. She still felt embarrassed and frustrated that she couldn't manage to figure it out herself. She wasn't sure if she could chalk all of it up to sleep deprivation and stress. After all, she was used to finding workarounds and brute forcing her way around the billionaire's systems with ease, cheating her away around the technology and exploiting its flaws rather than solving his puzzles and playing into his games. Perhaps beating people at their own game was a talent Daisy wasn't even aware she had. Figuring out how to appease people, play into their expectations, get them to trust her, find out how they think and crack their psychology wide open...manipulation? It sounded bad when she put it *that* way, didn't it? Really, though, it was badass. Daisy saw it as a sign of weakness, no doubt, was maybe even ashamed of it...but it was far more productive and took a hell of a lot more strategy than just solving every problem with tech and stealth.

And maybe Daisy felt the exact opposite way, she considered.

The password was correct. She didn't have to worry about forcing her way past the hard drive's password protection without triggering any potential security protocols. She felt envious. She wished she were better at social engineering and worming her way into people's heads, but she was not. Not even with people she's known and loathed for years on end.

There was one folder on top of the desktop's vivid sea of error-screen blue. It was left unnamed. "CLASSIFIED INFOR-MATION," the wallpaper's white text read. "USERS OF THIS SYSTEM REQUIRE STRICT AUTHORIZATION. VIOLAT-ERS WILL BE PERSECUTED."

Persecuted? Veronica thought, smiling to herself. *Did he mean prosecuted? Violaters?* If there was anything she was able to glean from that system at first glance, it was a fact that always managed to make itself apparent anywhere she went– the billionaire is a fucking idiot. He must have been the only person to ever use that drive, or in the least, only a very tight-knit group consisting of him and a couple of other people could access its contents. Anyone else would have known how to spell "violator" and would have known that "prosecuted" was the word he was look-ing for. Not to mention its overall amateurish user interface.

Then again, she thought with a sigh, *He* did *get one over on me with the periodic table encryption.* She winced in embarrassment at her failure to figure out such an escape room level code. Her obsession with her failure exposed her own fragile ego to herself, and that was not a good feeling either.

She opened the folder. There were only a couple documents inside of it. One was a text file, and the other, at least from its thumbnail, seemed to be...a map? She decided to examine the text file first.

It was encrypted using Base64. She smacked her hand against her forehead. Her ego came back with a vengeance.

Seriously? Of all the encryption methods you could have chosen, you chose middle schooler's first secret message? You might as well have used the Caesar shift.

She felt inadequate again. That only made her feel more incompetent about needing someone's help to decode the password. She was alternating between self-righteousness and self-hatred so fast, she couldn't keep up.

The laptop didn't have internet connection, so she painstakingly typed the message into a (very easily accessible, she might add) decoder.

When it spat out a new message, her mouth parted slightly in disbelief. She squinted at the screen.

...This motherfucker DID use the Caesar shift.

She smacked her hand against her forehead again, then translated it one more time. Contempt was quickly replaced with awe as she read the message in plain text.

If you're reading this, it means that I've passed away. What a bummer.

Jokes aside-- I'm so proud of you. You've done so well.

When I first met you, I was quite antsy about investing in your endeavors. No one else was picking up your projects. You were hard-headed, ambitious, even a bit crude...but something about the passion with which you spoke about Axis spoke to me. It was one of the riskiest decisions I've made in my career, and you've more than ensured that it's paid off.

When I was going over who should inherit my things, I was seriously considering letting this secret die with me. After all, I never got the damned thing to work. But I see something special in you. You've surpassed me, kid. I know you'll be the one to figure it out.

As for your partner, I think we can both agree that this should remain confidential. This is a gift from me to you nd to nobody else. Take this as my last piece of advice to you-- don't let just anyone see what's in your hand. Play your cards carefully, just as I have by entrusting you with this information.

Let's keep this man to man, alright?

Make me proud.

-C

She pressed her thumb to her lips and rested her chin on her hand, deep in thought. So he'd kept whatever this was a secret from everyone for this long. Why? Did the billionaire ever get any use out of it?

She navigated to the map. To her surprise, it was far more enlightening than the text file. It wasn't *just* a map, as the thumbnail had shown. There was an entire page of information included in the file, as well. She couldn't read it as it was, of course— it, too, was translated into Base64, presumably after being put through the Caesar shift.

Upon first glance, she found that the map was of the billionaire's island. She winced. *But it's all burned down, now.* She did not recognize anything on the map at all, which was full of representations of strange pathways and giant buildings. Maybe he'd destroyed it all a long time ago. She decided to translate all of the text before she made any assumptions.

INFORMATION ON ISIDORE 64, U.C.S. (UNDERGROUND COMPUTING SYSTEM), the information page's title read.

So she was incorrect. It wasn't that those structures no longer existed. They were all beneath the surface. It all clicked. Perhaps that's where the billionaire retrieved his other systems' power supply: but clearly, they were not one in the same. According to the map, this system was several kilometers underneath the island, reinforced with structures that the billionaire wouldn't have even thought to consider using. As she scrolled through the page, she found passwords, instructions for access, and most intriguing of all, speculation on what the Isidore 64 actually *was*.

NOTES FROM CHARLES:

THE ISIDORE 64 IS WHAT MUST BE ASSUMED TO BE A SUPER QUANTUM COMPUTING MACHINE. DESPITE WHAT ITS NAME MAY SUGGEST, I HAVE FOUND THAT IT IS A NEAR IMPOSSIBILITY THAT THIS COMPUTER FUNCTIONS USING CONVENTIONAL BITS. QUANTUM BITS SEEM EXPONENTIALLY MORE PLAUSIBLE.

WHAT WE ARE ABLE TO RESEARCH WITH THIS COMPUTER IS HIGHLY LIMITED. ADMITTEDLY, WE ARE UNABLE TO UNDERSTAND WHAT LITTLE INFORMATION IS ACCESSIBLE TO US. FOR THE MOST PART, WE ARE FORCED TO TAKE A BEHAVIORIST APPROACH IN OUR RESEARCH. WE KNOW THAT THE COMPUTER HAS NAMED ITSELF. WE KNOW THAT

IT IS CAPABLE OF CRAFTING HIGH-LEVEL PUNS (HENCE ITS NAME.) WE ALSO KNOW THAT THE COMPUTER EXHIBITS THE TRAITS OF A COMPLEX SECURITY SYSTEM. IT HAS HUMAN LIKE PRECISION, AS IF IT IS CONSIDERING WHAT INFORMATION ITS USERS SHOULD HAVE ACCESS TO IN REAL TIME.

THE COMPUTER WILL CONVERSE WITH US CONSISTENTLY ON THE SAME LEVEL AS A PERSON. NO MATTER WHAT WE TYPE INTO IT, IT NEVER GIVES AN IMPROPER RESPONSE. IT HAS A DISTINCT PERSONALITY THAT REMAINS CONSISTENT REGARDLESS OF USER INPUT, WHICH GIVES US PAUSE AS TO WHETHER THIS COMPUTER LEARNS BASED OFF OF USER INPUT.

THIS MACHINE IS ENTIRELY OTHERWORLDLY. ORIGIN UNKNOWN.

NOTES FROM ME:

EXTENSIVE CONVERSATION WITH CHARLES AND "ISIDORE" HAS REVEALED THAT THIS MACHINE HAS CAPABILITIES RELEVANT TO MY GOALS SO LONG AS I AM ABLE TO HARNESS ITS POWER. IMPOSSIBLE, THUS FAR.

SORRY, CHARLES.

I'LL KEEP TRYING. I DO NOT NECESSARILY AGREE WITH THE IDEA THAT ISIDORE IS A QUANTUM COMPUTER.

IT WILL NOT ALLOW US TO REMOVE ITS PROTECTIVE PAN-ELING, SO THERE IS NO WAY TO TELL. I LOVE CHARLES LIKE A FATHER, BUT THE GUY'S OLD AND HAS SOME OUTDATED IDEAS ON WHAT COMPLEX COMPUTING LOOKS LIKE. IT DOES NOT OPERATE ON BITS. I DOUBT IT EVEN OPERATES ON QUBITS.

THAT SAID, I HAVE NO CLUE HOW ISIDORE OPERATES. I'D ALMOST THINK IT WAS A REAL PERSON PLAYING A MAS-SIVE PRANK ON US IF I DIDN'T KNOW ANY BETTER.

WHAT I SEE IN ISIDORE IS A WAY OUT. I KNOW FOR CERTAIN THAT THE COMPUTER IS ABLE TO TRANSPORT OUR CONSCIOUSNESS INTO SIMULATED WORLDS. THAT IS A BREAKTHROUGH I MADE THAT CHARLES WAS NEVER ABLE TO. IT WAS TERRIFYING.

I UNDERSTAND THAT IT IS IMPOSSIBLE FOR A COM-PUTER TO HAVE FEELINGS, BUT I CAN ALMOST SWEAR THAT IT HAS BECOME VINDICTIVE TOWARD ME. IF I CAN HARNESS THIS TECHNOLOGY, I CAN BECOME THE GOD OF METAWORLD. ISIDORE ALREADY HAS ACCESS TO IT. I JUST NEED TO MAKE THAT FINAL CONNECTION.

THIS IS MY LIFEBOAT. THE FUTURE FEELS UNCERTAIN. NOBODY ELSE CAN KNOW ABOUT THIS.

Veronica slumped back in her chair, bringing her hands to

her face. They were shaking, curled up, grasping at nothing but cold dusty air.

She glanced behind her. Nobody was there.

There was one last thing that Veronica needed to secure, she remembered. She shuffled in one of her drawers, then produced a black case– also secured with a combination lock, such a childish attempt to protect herself, the same thing they use for *high schoolers' lockers,* for God's sake.

It hadn't been put to use in so long. Not since she was Xanthippe. Muscle memory kicked in as she lifted her automatic out of its case, loaded it, then turned the safety off all in one motion. Cocked it. Pointed it at the computer. Pressed the trigger. Watched the screen tear into pieces. She switched her aim toward the hard drive. It cracked, exposing all of its gold-and-teal innards. Copper-freckled chips exploded across her floor. The metallic clicks of scattering hardware and shattered glass sounded like high-pitched, pleading screams beneath the unforgiving drum of firing bullets.

She shoved the gun into the waistband of her briefs, beads of perspiration forming on her forehead. She'd just showered, but could still smell her own body odor every time she lifted her arms. It was a specific hormonal soupy stench of nervous sweat, not from exercising, not from overexertion, but from pure fear.

She picked up a piece of hard drive. Snapped it in half. Did that over and over again until nothing remained. Burnt the paper, the folders, all of it.

Drool dripped down the corner of her mouth. She wiped it off with the back of her hand, never taking her eyes off of the scuffed black spot on the smooth floor where there once was a hard drive. Her stomach tightened. She no longer had any information to offer in exchange for her freedom. That was it. She was of no use to *them* anymore. What did that mean for her?

The human brain is the best encryption device of all, yet people always spoil its power by opening their mouths. She cracked a grin. *They know that regardless of everything I destroyed, I still have information they want. Now there's no way for them to find it without me.*

They can kill me, but they'll have to track me down first. Question me first. Bribe me. Torture me.

And I will never tell them anything.

18

WITHDRAW

The clicking of her grandmother's crochet needles prevented Daisy from getting too sucked into the sitcom they were watching together. Not that there was much substance to get invested in, anyway– but it was a nice break from the true crime shows that her grandmother liked to watch most other times. Daisy kicked her feet up. Sounds of guns firing and husky-voiced narrators replaced with bad dates and terrible one-liners. She smirked and wondered if that was *actually* any better.

It had been a few days since she last spoke with Veronica. It took her some time to find it in her to relax a little again. Last she heard, the password worked. *Everything's going to be fine,* Veronica had assured her. She sounded stilted. More nervous than usual. It shook Daisy up quite a lot, to say the least. Everything felt like an attempt to distract herself. Most of them failed. The smirk faded from her face as her current attempt failed, as well.

It wasn't even anxiety about her own world, really. She'd been in constant fear that something bad may happen– anything– even before she learned that she was living in a universe inside of a computer run by a cruel, chauvinist god. Sure, she didn't want to *add* to that anxiety, so she certainly didn't want to hear about anything happening outside of her universe that might put everything she holds dear in jeopardy. But that was the thing. She also held *Veronica* dear. Daisy did not know what was going on with Veronica's government, with the state of Metaworld's protection and security, none of that. What she *did* know was that her friend was acting unstable and strange. That her friend was living in fear. She'd also considered the fact that Veronica's word is not gospel. She was a person, and she was not infallible. Perhaps her responsibilities were crushing her, making her imagine threats out of paranoia. Hell, Daisy didn't know if *she* would be able to handle that kind of responsibility, after all.

"You thinking hard. What's up?" Her grandmother's dark, frail voice interrupted her train of thought.

"Nothing," she murmured, self-conscious of just how *posed* she'd become. She looked strained and intense. She lifted her chin out of her hands and sat up straight.

"Okay, okay, won't pry." Her tone was jovial and teasing. She must have still thought that Daisy had someone *special* she wasn't telling her about yet.

The television screen fatigued her. Her eyelids began to droop as she was both hypnotized by the T.V. and grew bored with it at the same time. When she lost the struggle and they dropped over her pupils at last, she fell asleep without hesitation.

It was one of those rare moments where her dreams decided

to comfort her. When she opened her eyes again, she was standing in the middle of a park. The fragrance of those ever-familiar white strawberries wafted across her nose. Everything looked low-quality and grainy, like she was viewing the world around her through the lens of a home video or a CRT television. The sky above her bloomed in gorgeous shades of rose instead of the familiar indigo-red she was used to. How did time work in this dreamscape? Perhaps it was earlier in the afternoon than normal? As always, the weather was perfect. No pairs of broken glasses were anywhere to be found– any other time, they would have signaled to Daisy that she was in a dream. After all, she doesn't *wear* glasses. But that time, she knew she was dreaming from the moment she fell asleep.

A tall figure blackened with shadow stood in the distance. She could not tell if it was staring right at her or if it was turned away, but she still recognized its silhouette.

"Veronica?" she attempted. Her voice came out as a hoarse whisper. The figure did not seem to hear her.

Daisy *hated* when that happened– when her dreams made her so helpless. She breathed in, breathed out, cleared her throat, then tried again. "Veronica!" she shouted. Her voice boomed across the clearing like a bullet exploding out of a pistol. Birds burst out of the strawberry bushes, scolded her with their harsh, nasally trills, then disappeared as if the sky swallowed them whole. Her echo fell into the distance and skipped across the ground like a stone on a river. Veronica shifted and walked toward her. It didn't look like she was getting anywhere– she just seemed to be walking in place– but before Daisy knew it, she was standing right behind her. Veronica still said nothing.

"Veronica," Daisy breathed, "is it really you? Or is this just a weird dream?"

"Isn't it always me?" Her voice was hoarse. Her curls looked dry and crunchy, and her lips were lined with red-and-white cracks. Dried drool left a trail of white crust down her chin. She was dressed down, her white shirt soaked with pungent sweat, the waistband of her underwear poking out above her pants. Emanating off of her was the infused stench of technology and thick human secretion. Heat, silicon, metal. Burnt plastic. Gunpowder. Fear.

"What's wrong with you?"

"I need you to hear me out," she said, ignoring Daisy's question. "I need to do something to you."

Daisy blinked.

"I need to put you away. Things are getting bad. Really bad. I just learned some new information, and maybe...maybe I can find a way to use it?" She broke into humorless giggles, putting her palm up to her perspiration-soaked forehead. "Yeah. It's my best bet. I need to put you back in a chip. It's for your protection. To save you. And...it won't *feel* like anything, you know, you'll just...wake up like nothing has ever happened, worst comes to worst, things might just...change for you a little. And that's the worst case scenario."

She squinted in response, her mouth slightly agape. "Veronica," she repeated, "what is *wrong with you?*"

"You asked me not to tell you," she responded impatiently. "Look, just trust me. I said I'm always going to protect you–"

"You said you're always going to protect my *world*. And what about everyone else? You're not going to put *them* in a chip too?"

"I can. I can!" she interrupted, looking into Daisy's eyes. Her red-rimmed scleras were wild and pleading. "I can...I can download your grandma onto a chip, anyone else you want, too, just name them!"

"But that's not protecting my *world*. That's just protecting the people close to *me*. What about the billions of other people in my world? Do they not matter, too?" The sky began to darken. "And what if your plan fails? Then we're just going to stay in those chips forever, never to be alive again. Is that *really* protecting us? Or just protecting our potential, Veronica?" Daisy stepped closer to her. "You need to really think about what you're about to do."

"I *have* thought about it!" she responded with exasperation. "It's your best bet. And I *can't lose you.* You're one of the most important things to me."

She looked up at her, narrowing her eyes. "You're important to me too. It kills me to see you like this. But when you made a promise to protect this entire world–" she gestured to the quickly-fading landscape– "I took that to heart. It's either all of us or none of us. You can't pick and choose and only take some of us. I'm fucking exhausted of being plucked out of my world." Her voice cracked. "Being stuck in a chip...that's nothingness. Pure nothingness. No good, no bad, no experiences at all. What's the point of existing?"

"I know, I know, I understand what you're getting at. But this is different!" She clutched Daisy by the shoulders. "I *will* make sure you get to exist again or else I wouldn't be doing this. I already *had* this revelation, Daisy. I copied your old self onto a chip before I imported you back into your universe." She averted her eyes in shame. "But then...then I realized something. by keeping the *old* you stored away, I was just being selfish. Hoarding a version of you that no longer really existed. And I got rid of the chip. Because *you,* the you that you've become, that's who matters."

The landscape that was previously fading to black began to change to deep scarlet.

"You downloaded me onto a chip," Daisy rasped, "then you *got rid of it?* Destroyed it, right?"

Her eyes widened. "What else was I meant to do?"

"How could you be so fucking cold?" She pushed Veronica away. Her grip fell away from Daisy's shoulders, causing her to trip over her own feet. Veronica collapsed onto the ground and stared up at Daisy in horror. Her eyes were filled with icy hatred. "Just picking and choosing versions of me? Fucking around with my– no, my *world's* existence? What if you stop liking *me,* huh? You just gonna load a different version of me? Kill the old me? Because that's what's convenient for *you?"*

She'd never seen Daisy so enraged before. Veronica balled her hands into fists, still in shock, unable to look away from her rage-contorted face. Her stomach felt like it was full of stones. "Daisy," she whispered, "it's not like that. *I'm* not like that. Please–"

"You insist that you're not a god, then you do this kind of shit to me? What the fuck are you playing at?" Her rasp turned into a throaty scream. The red that surrounded them turned more vibrant with every word she spat. Her pupils contracted in response to both the color's growing intensity and the adrenaline flooding her body. They bloomed back to their normal size when realization hit her. She began to whisper again. "No, no, no...It's not that you like this version of me better, is it?" Daisy put her head in her hands. "It's that I'm the version who can tell you about the billionaire. Give you all of the information you need on him." Her eyes darted back over to Veronica's face. Daisy looked sick and pale. "Be a *shoulder to cry on*. Isn't that right?"

Veronica averted Daisy's gaze. Her eyes welled up with tears. For a few seconds that felt like hours, thick silence lay between them. "You don't understand. It wasn't...*all* because of that," she whispered. "I've grown to really care–"

"Shut up," Daisy croaked. She felt that familiar build-up of mucus and shrillness in her throat. She never was able to control it. "You just see me as an object. I just exist to serve you, don't I? I should have known better than to get attached to you. You're just like him. I wish that you *never* overwrote me, that I was still just as oblivious to this...*bullshit* as I was before. I wish I never met you." She took a deep breath. "Get the fuck out of my dream."

Everything collapsed in on itself and formed a singularity.

Daisy woke up screaming.

19

UNLOCK

She tossed her headset to the side. Nothing felt real. She looked down at her own shaky hands. She was barely even able to pinch her pointer finger and her thumb together to unzip her suit. Her vision blurred, unblurred, blurred again back and forth.

Veronica's eyes darted up to the projector above her. She turned it off.

All of the units in the room buzzed and hummed, sounding as if they were whispering to one another, watching the scene with bated breath. Gossiping about her. Judging her. It was eerily quiet– too quiet. How long had she been in Metaworld for?

She felt an odd presence.

Who was watching her right then? Or was she just imagining it? She couldn't afford to assume that anything was just her imagination, she realized. She placed one hand on her gun's grip and used the other to pull her phone out of the tinfoil bag she'd been keeping it in. With bomb detonation-like caution, she turned it off airplane mode. She couldn't stay in that room anymore. Not around Daisy. Not around whoever was watching her. She winced as she typed ever so slowly with just one thumb. Her hands were shaking, half out of anxiety and half out of fever overtaking her body. After what felt like hours of typing, she took a deep breath and sent the message.

i need u. please come and get me. i cant be locked up in here anymore. dont take me home. dont take me to your house. drive me somewhere far away. trust me.

Tears dropped onto her phone's screen, warping the words glowing through it like a small and fruitless beacon.

He began typing. She held her breath.

...

I'm with my kids.

More tears fell. She let out a choked grunt. Just as she was about to throw her phone on the ground and fill it with bullets, he began typing again. She let go of her gun to grasp her phone with both hands, squatting down to the ground. Heavy breaths climbed up and down her lungs. Her shoulders hunched forward as she strained to prevent herself from becoming light-headed.

...

Give me a few more minutes to spend with them. I will be there.

She broke down into sobs as soon as she finished reading that message. Whoever was watching her, *if* they were watching her, would have quite the pathetic sight to behold. A grown woman with her kind of experience, always over-competent, bold, strong, reduced to a watery mess by a text message. Perhaps they were right about her. Everyone. Daisy included. How was she really any better than her predecessor? Did she hate him because she saw herself in him? He was self-centered, egotistical, opportunistic, predatory...

I should have known better than to get attached to you. You're just like him.

If only Daisy knew that she really did care about her all along.

Perhaps the billionaire felt the exact same way. Maybe in his own sick and twisted way, he *did* feel love for Daisy. Or maybe that feeling was a perverted cousin of love. Not true love.

Did Veronica truly care about Daisy?

Maybe not at first, she reasoned. No, not at first for sure. Daisy was right in that regard. But she cared about her the same way she cared about anybody else. What Daisy didn't understand was that the way Veronica treated her was not because she was simulated, not because she saw her as less human for the mere fact she lived in a little self-contained world of her own. It was because that's how Veronica had always treated everybody for a very long time. As a means to an end. And after Daisy lashed out at her, she realized just how much her own egocentrism isolated her from the rest of the world. She never considered the idea that people do care about her, value her opinion, and value the way she treats them. So she'd fucked up with Nancy, with Josiah, and now with Daisy. She'd only been successful in pushing everyone away from her, perpetuating a lonely cycle oiled with her own feeling of insignificance and worthlessness. Doing nothing but digging her heels into her socially awkward nature, getting herself into trouble with her complete lack of awareness. It didn't make her logical, or calculated, or smarter than anyone else. It made her a shitty human being.

Her back pressed against the cold floor as she waited for Josiah and passed the time with mini epiphanies. She stared up at the ceiling, high and impressive and authoritative in its brutalist architecture. Where had her authority gone? Who had she become?

She glanced back down at her phone and thought of her father. Her breath caught in her throat. Veronica hadn't even thought of her *father's* safety through all of this. Had he been receiving strange messages? Threats? Would they target him to try and get to her? Why hadn't she considered that before? Of course, he hadn't reached out to her, and Veronica followed the mentality that no news was good news.

But maybe it was time.

With hesitance, she pressed the call button and held it up to her ear.

"Hello?" a husky voice crackled out. He sounded about as tipsy as he usually would be during that time of day. "Who is this?"

He doesn't even have my new number saved, she thought. *That's how little we talk.* That alone was enough to make her eyes gloss over again.

"Dad," she whispered, "It's me. Ronnie."

It was quiet for a moment. She thought she could hear her father grunting as he sat down somewhere. The ever-familiar sound of ice clinking against glass managed to make its way to his microphone.

"Ronnie," he said. "Hi, sweetie. What's up? Is everything okay?"

She swallowed. "Yeah, Dad. Just wanted to say hi. See what you're up to."

"You're not too busy saving the world?" He chuckled under his breath, dry and gruff. "I'm just joshing. I know you're a busy lady. I mean, I haven't been up to anything that would impress ya..."

"No. I think it would. Really. Tell me about your day." She tried not to let her voice betray the deep melancholy boring into her chest.

"Well," he started, "I had a job interview today. I know what you're gonna say, and I still don't want any money from you. Not the kind of guy to mooch off his little girl, no matter how much she has, right? And it's not like I've *earned* that right either. You practically raised yourself. I want to keep *some* of my dignity, at least. Anyway. I think things went really well. I don't see any more odd gigs and shitty bosses in my future."

"That's great, Dad," she rasped through a pained smile. "Hey, uh. By the way. Have you noticed anything weird? Any weird messages, emails, anyone trying to...contact you in any way?"

"Nope. Not from anyone but Nigerian princes and hot singles in my area. Why, Ron?"

"No reason," she said, her tone a little more strained than she meant it to be. "I mean, people are...weird toward public figures like me, y'know? Just wanted to make sure they aren't tracking you down to try and get to me."

"Ah. Fans. I see. Pretty lady like you? You've gotta have some stalkers, huh? After all, you *do* take after my good looks."

Veronica grinned. A scoff escaped her nose.

"Well," he chuckled, "I'm not too worried about *you*, Ronnie. I know that security is your thing. And what would they want with an old paunchy man like me? Especially one with a gun?" He laughed again. Softer, this time. "I can take care of myself. Ya don't gotta worry about me."

Her phone vibrated.

Here, the message read.

"I've got something I need to take care of," Veronica finished. "I can't keep them waiting. I'm sorry. I wish we could've talked longer–"

"No, no. Don't worry about that. I'm happy we got to talk at all. I'll talk to you later, alright? Go on and do what you do."

"Okay. Bye, Dad," she breathed.

"I'm proud of you. Now get out there and show them who's boss. Goodbye."

Three tones denoted that the call was over.

—

An awkwardness hung in the air when Veronica collapsed in the back seat of the car. Not just awkwardness. Something else, too. A strange sense of tragedy that was so heavy, she could feel it resting on her shoulders. Josiah did not even glance at her from his rearview, did not even act as if he noticed whenever she got in the car. When she looked at him in the mirror, caught a glimpse of just his eyes, she did not see the same kind of focused rage that she witnessed when she arrived late after dancing with Daisy. Instead, there was a thousand-yard stare. A softened expression of regret and pain. Did he think she'd become a lost cause? Did he find her just as pathetic as she found herself? Perhaps, she thought, he was grieving the person that he once thought she was. The Xanthippe to his Whiskey, that commandeering movie spy-like personality that she donned for the sake of the greater good and shed like a second skin the moment she walked through her apartment's doorway. That person must have been dead to him, and the final nail in the coffin was Veronica asking him to help her run away. She was pathetic. Smelled like dirt and sweat and failure.

Or maybe, she thought, she shouldn't think of herself as that important to him. He had his own life outside of her. Maybe something was going on outside of work. Maybe he couldn't give a shit that she was about to leave for God knows where, never to return. It would be understandable.

As if answering her thoughts, Josiah at last shot a look at her. That look was *pointed.* Painted on his face in direct response to her. She could see it in the way he winced as he averted his eyes just as soon as he'd rested them on her. As if he'd touched a hot stove by mistake.

"Josiah," she tried, "how are the kids doing?"

"They're fine." Curt and snappy.

"Are you okay?"

"I'm fine. Just...stop asking me questions. Please. I don't want to talk about it. Or anything."

So she didn't. Her insides felt like they were rotting. Nobody cared about her anymore, and she brought it on herself by acting so damn selfish. Their message thread would be the last time she asked him for anything. Probably he was glad to be rid of her.

They drove for hours. The sun set behind the trees, then made itself apparent again when the trees and beige suburbs circling L.A. thinned out into sparse shacks. Then nothing. Cracked, yellow-white desert spread wide and flat in front of them like a tablecloth. It would have burned even hotter outside if it wasn't for the sun's cautious afternoon hike back down the horizon. Much to the relief of everything in California that was forced to live beneath it.

"Thanks for doing this." It was the first thing Veronica said since they first left the parking lot. There was no response from Josiah.

About thirty minutes later, the doors clicked. Josiah had locked them.

Then he began to speak.

"You're aware by now that there are important people after you."

She blinked in shock. *How does he know?* Chills trickled down her spine. "Yeah. I tried to protect you from–"

"You're not in a good spot. Do you understand the gravity of your situation?" His tone was flat. Like a disappointed father.

"I do," she croaked. "I really do."

"As we speak, there are swarms of very powerful people that want more than anything for you to be dead. Who are willing to do anything to make that death happen." Beads of sweat misted his skin. Lost in concentration, he pressed the gas pedal harder. They barreled down the barren road.

Nobody around for miles, Veronica thought dully.

"I know," she replied. "That's why I asked you to help me. How do you know all of th–"

"Because, *Xanthippe*," he spat, "I'm the one who is leading you to them."

Without thinking, she snatched her gun out of her pants and planted its muzzle against the back of his head. *"Don't do this,"* she hissed, half threat, half plea.

The gas pedal was almost pressed flat against the floor. He didn't even steal a glimpse at the pair of wild eyes that would have greeted him in his rearview mirror. "If you shoot me, we will both die," he explained. His tone remained even and eerie. "This vehicle has a dead man's switch built into it." Still keeping one hand gripped tight around the steering wheel, he lifted his shirt. His skin was clammy and pale, looked sticky to the touch. An electrode rested over his heart. Veronica's eyes trailed down to the wire attached to it. It snaked onto the floor and looped into the car's body. "If I get out of this driver's seat without permission, the electrode will tear off, it will activate the bomb housed under this car's hood, and it will explode. The second I leave the vehicle, it will explode. The second..." He took a deep breath that sounded like a death rattle. "The second my heart stops, we are both as good as dead." He was cracking.

"Are they listening to us?" she demanded.

"Yes."

She unlocked her elbow and took her finger off of the trigger, but she did not move the gun away from his head. "I can't believe you're doing this," she muttered.

Josiah grew even more frustrated. The car was going faster by the second. She heard its engine cry out, watched the speedometer's needle crawl upward, looking as if it were going to go full circle. *Like a child on a swing set,* she thought with no amusement. *A child on a swing set trying to go all the way around.*

"You were the one asking me about my kids earlier," he hissed. "You *know* I have a family to go home to. Who knows what they'd do to them if I don't do this? Have you even thought about what they might do to what little family *you* have left, Veronica? Or are you too self-centered for that?"

"You're not the one with the upper hand here. Be careful how you speak."

She was tempted to slip her pointer back over the trigger and press the gun harder into his skull. Shake him up a little more. Instead, she squeezed the grip tighter.

"Do you know how nerve-wracking it's been? Waiting to be put in the line of duty? Knowing that eventually, they were going to force me into this, and it was just a matter of *when?*"

Veronica blinked in shock. "How long ago were you put up to this?" she whispered.

"There's still a chance," he continued, ignoring her question. "For both of us. Taking you in for questioning doesn't mean certain death. You just need to cooperate with them. Tell them what they want to hear." He sighed. "I can't...keep doing what I used to. I have kids. I *need* to do this."

"I can't just cooperate with them," Veronica said, holding back tears. "I destroyed all of the information they'd want from me. And I *don't regret it.* I will never contribute my technology to a government that only wants it so they can use it against people like me. I'm not that person, Josiah. I don't fucking pull up ladders from underneath me." Her voice intensified into a scream. "I will never support those corrupt fascists. *Never.* Not over my dead fucking body. I can't. I'm sorry. They can do whatever they want to me, and I will never tell them what they want to hear. They can take anything away from me." She thought of Daisy. "But the rest of the world's too important, even if I'm not in it anymore. Guess I lost sight of that."

"Oh, Veronica," Josiah breathed.

She lifted the automatic away from his skull. "For what it's worth," she choked out, her voice wavering, "I never planned on actually shooting you anyway." She tearfully chuckled and turned the gun's safety off. "See?" she smiled. Then she pressed it to her head.

"Veronica!" Josiah screamed. He slammed on the car's brakes. The weapon slipped from her grasp and her head smacked against the back of the passenger's seat. Her ears rang.

"Get out. Get the fuck out of the car now." He whipped around and slipped a folded piece of paper between her fingers.

"Huh-"

"Fucking run! Get out! Go, Xanthippe!"

She grabbed her gun's handle and smashed the window with it, thrusting her entire body forward. The sharp, gritty pain exploding across her fist was the only reminder that any of what was happening was real. It felt like she was in a dream where everything happened in slow motion. She was suspended in the air, parallel to the dusty road that lay beneath her, preemptively sore as she waited for her body to collide with it. At first, she thought only she could hear the odd ringing sound. Then it turned into high-pitched beeps lined up in rapid succession. Growing faster. She stumbled back up and sprinted.

She did not take three strides before everything erupted, heat baking her back, her entire body heaving far across the ground. Without a second thought, she stood up again. The adrenaline took it from there.

20

FATHER

He's gone.

She darted across the sand, her torso barely able to keep up with her legs. Her lips were cracked and her tongue felt like cotton. It felt like sucking pure heat through a straw as she strained to breathe, letting out a whimper with every exhale. Her singed t-shirt flapped behind her in the wind.

He was really gone.

The sheet of paper he'd given her fluttered in her hands. She hadn't looked at it yet–first she had to flee the scene, and she felt like she could not get far enough away from it. Then she realized that there would be nothing she could use for miles. She must have been somewhere around Death Valley. Close to the United States. Perhaps Josiah was meant to take her to Nevada. If she kept running, did she just increase her risk of running into border patrol?

She fell to her knees and broke out into full-blown sobs again. She wanted to just die and get it all over with. Let all of the information they ever could have gotten their hands on dissipate. Sure, maybe they'd question her employees and piece *some* of it together, but certainly not all of it. If it were that easy, they would not have resorted to such drastic measures. Veronica, Josiah, and the billionaire were the only ones with access to those final puzzle pieces that had the potential to create some of the deadliest, most powerful technology in the world. *And two of those people are dead now. I could be the third, and there would be absolutely zero chance of them finding out.*

But Josiah didn't want her to die, did he? He could have sold her out. Secured his own safety. Let her shoot herself in the back of his car, could have delivered her dead body, divulged what little he knew, even if it didn't amount to all of the secrets Veronica had access to, made it out clean...but he didn't. For some reason that was completely alien to Veronica right then, he sacrificed his own life so she could continue her meager existence.

Before she made any final decisions about killing herself, she unfolded the sheet of paper and scanned it, trying not to let her tears soak the already sweaty and grime-thin page.

Veronica,

Run NORTH from the explosion site for about five miles. Do not stop running after you've read this message. You will come across something that will help you. Keep an eye out. They could be any-where, and they will have the area surrounded soon after my death. Stay ready to fight.

You must live. You were right to destroy everything. We can't let them have access to it. I can't let my kids live in the type of society they are trying to create. The world already hates them enough. Regardless, your knowledge and Axis's tech is invaluable. So you need to hang on to it. Treat yourself like the Library of Alexandria. For the love of God, do not burn down.

Put what you know in the right hands, Veronica. Give it to someone who will use it to do right by my family. By everyone on this planet. By you.

I've served my purpose. Destroy this note.

She didn't know how she had it in her through the dehydration, but she managed to produce even more tears than before. She sniffed and folded the note back up, then rolled it into a tube. She attempted to swallow it whole. She gagged. It felt like she was shoving a knife down her own throat. She had no saliva, no water, nothing to force it down with. Hands shaking, she took it back out of her mouth, tore it into quarters, and painstakingly swallowed them one at a time. Then she slipped one foot flat on the ground, hoisted herself back up, and sprinted once again.

—

That catchy late-1900s song about walking a thousand miles was stuck in her head. She could feel herself growing delirious with every new puff of dust her foot produced, every new pang of thirst, every stupid lyric from some stupid American folk song that refused to wriggle its way out of her brain. She felt absolutely mindless. Like a shark wading toward its prey, not knowing anything except that it needs to survive. Like a shark that needs to distract itself from its friend's death with old tunes, now that it's run out of tears to cry. She thought it strange and irrational, all the ways the human mind self-soothed in the most dire of situations.

The mud cracks grew so wide she thought that her foot would get caught in one of them if she wasn't careful. Dodging them felt like a game. *The floor is lava. Step on a crack–* she winced. She never got over her sensitivity to that childish turn of phrase. It was embarrassing to remember how angry she'd get with the other children on the playground for so much as uttering *break your mama's back.* She thought it was some weird conspiracy against her to tease her about her deceased mother. She came by her paranoia honestly, she guessed.

She craved water like she'd never craved it before. What's more, a stitch was slicing into her side. Her left shoulder threw itself down in pain. If she had anything in her to vomit other than paper, she might have. It was a hard pill to swallow, but she just wasn't as athletic as she was back when the billionaire was still alive. Of course, it could also be chalked up to the fact that she was in Death-fucking-Valley, that she had no water to drink, hadn't eaten, whatever else...but really, it was easy to imagine her old self being able to run those five miles, no problem. Sprint them the whole way, even. Water and food or not. Probably in a half hour, too.

Veronica must have been running for close to thirty minutes by then, actually. She realized that she'd been staring at the ground the entire time, growing motion-sick on top of the regular sick. What the hell was she doing? She'd focused so much on trying not to trip, song lyrics, stupid childhood memories, that she was no longer really paying attention to where she was going. What was wrong with her? She was supposed to function at her finest under pressure, yet she was slipping so hard.

She lifted her head. Across the vast nothingness was a black speck. Her eyes narrowed. From that distance, she could not make it out. Her stomach flipped. Whatever that thing was, it must have been what Josiah left behind for her. It couldn't have been a person, wasn't a building, nothing like that. Maybe some kind of vehicle? She didn't think it was an enemy. She'd managed to get by without any encounters so far. That was good.

Her thought was interrupted. The sound of a gun firing cracked across the distance. She'd jinxed herself. She yelped and looked over her shoulder. Someone was trailing her.

"Stop! Don't resist! Get down on the ground!"

She ducked and picked up her pace, stumbling her way across the muddy sand. Soon he'd call his buddies if he hadn't already. They would apprehend her with ease. She closed her eyes, took a deep breath, and placed both hands on her weapon. The man was about a hundred yards away. It wouldn't be an easy shot, and he had to be just as experienced with his gun as Veronica was with hers. She held her breath, twisted to the side, and fired, never slowing her pace.

She shot him right through the head. He fell backwards, cut off mid-shout. Veronica shuddered. She felt not a single ounce of satisfaction with her chillingly successful aim. Despite her training, despite the high-stakes missions she'd been on before, that was the first person she'd ever killed.

She'd only confirmed what the whole world thought of her. She'd become a murderer.

More footsteps behind her. More shouts, all bleeding into one another. Her ears rang. She grasped the cross pendant around her neck.

Hail Mary, full of grace.

One of them, a small woman, sprinted faster than all the others. She had sloppy aim, Veronica noticed. She could use that. She managed to dodge all of her bullets– not that it was that difficult, anyway. She looked young. Scared. What were they doing, sending a little girl like her on this mission? It was sick.

Veronica allowed her to get closer. She kept running toward her until she was only ten feet away at most. Her eardrums felt like they exploded when the girl fired one last shot. It managed to graze Veronica's shoulder. They likely had explicit orders not to shoot to kill, she recognized. In response, she shot the woman in the head. Guilt gnawed at her intestines.

Blessed art thou amongst women,

She hoisted her over her shoulders like a backpack and continued to run. Hot blood flowed down her back, soaking her shirt. The impact of bullets peppered her, but she did not feel any pain other than dull blows that would later become bruises. Her new shield took all of the brunt. The girl was wearing a bulletproof vest, just like all of her cohorts. That helped.

Veronica still wanted to throw up.

And blessed is the fruit of thy womb, Jesus.

The black speck soon turned into a small helicopter. Her chopper. Josiah had moved it for her. She never even noticed that it was gone. Too bad she was leading everyone behind her right to it, too. Encouraged by her newfound safe haven, just within arm's reach, her very last chance at surviving, she sprinted even faster than before. Her body seemed to entirely forget about the new weight that had been placed on it.

Holy Mary, Mother of God,

Nobody else managed to catch up with her before she reached it, but they were still mere yards away. She ducked behind it. There wasn't much time. She peeled off the woman's vest and strapped it to herself, then hoisted herself inside of the helicopter.

Pray for us sinners,

A stray bullet whizzed past her head as soon as she entered. She looked out of her open door and swore under her breath. They were filling her chopper with lead. Fruitlessly, she shot back with one hand as she made her way through the vehicle's security system. Finger prints, a retina scan, and password entry were all required before it would start. She reached up toward the generator switch on the roof. Pain exploded across her armpit just a moment afterward. She screamed. They took advantage of the unprotected, tender spot between her vest and her arm. She'd been shot.

Now and at the hour of our death.

It felt like a giant fist was crushing her ribcage. Squeezing blood out of her heart like it was juicing an orange. She half-wheezed, half-whimpered as she awkwardly pulled the cockpit door closed with her right arm and forced the aircraft to take off. Enraged grunts erupted from her throat every time her body shifted, hitting her with a new wave of tight pain. Her vision was blurry and she had no clue where she was going.

The island, she thought. *They can't follow me past the coast. And they don't know about the island's existence.*

It was so obvious. How had she not seen it before?

She rose to the sky with nauseating speed. It was a rocky takeoff, but she made it. She looked down at the group of agents collected where her helicopter rested before, still aiming their firearms at her, walkie-talkies up to their mouths. They soon turned into ants.

Amen.

21

ADMIRE

For then, her helicopter would be just about undetectable. She couldn't take all of the credit. After all, developing aircraft, let alone a stealth chopper, was far from her specialty. With some help from her team she'd managed to modify it to near invisibility. They'd taken notes from the United States' RAH-66 Comanche. Ironic, given her situation. They modernized its design, of course– instead of opting for a ducted tail rotor, they decided to modify it so it did not need one at all, and its fuel efficiency was severely lacking for the 2040s. Her team covered it with infrared-suppressant paint. Installed five blades instead of the original three. Her mouth twitched at the reminder of her old team. None of them remained. It was a small group, having five members at its height. But after they were all fired, many of them gave up on their mission. They had families to take care of. Had to retire from their frustration with the order of things after a while. Unlike Veronica, they had other things to worry about. They could only carry that rage in their hearts for so long before they had to let go.

Either that, or the negativity consumed them until they were pushed past their final breaking point.

Clover was the one who put in the most work on her aircraft. They were a scrappy little ex-combat pilot, fifty years old with a chip on their shoulder when they first joined the company. Veronica was tasked with putting them (and everyone else in that wave of new hires– a busy time, it was) through the onboarding process, but she wasn't the one who hired them or asked them to join her team. They were hired into the aeronautics department, a very small and distant section of Axis at the time. It wasn't the center of the billionaire's attention to say the least, but something he was interested in dipping his toes in regardless. Josiah was the person they grew closest with and divulged their angst about the world's corruption to, once they'd established enough trust with one another. It made sense. They were a little closer to one another in age, and they both had that same kind of *bite* to their personalities.

When Clover was modifying the aircraft, Veronica always managed to feel inadequate in their presence. Clover was exactly who she wanted to become in a few decades' time. In top physical shape, had mental fortitude like she'd never seen before. Small, but pushed all five feet of their body to their absolute limit. Unstoppable. Quick-witted: always had a response for everything. And if it weren't for what happened, perhaps Clover would have been the one who was more deserving of Veronica's position.

After they were fired, nobody heard from them for days.

Veronica thought that they were just taking the news a little hard. Needed some time to bounce back. It was Josiah who ventured to their apartment and found them splayed out on their floor, gun in hand.

When she first heard the news, Veronica refused to believe that Clover would have ever taken their own life. It was impossible— it couldn't have been them, she thought, someone must have killed them and covered it up. Even when Josiah assured her that he didn't think that was the case, that he truly believed they'd been pushed to their absolute brink, Veronica still could not fathom it at the time.

But now she could.

She took a deep breath. Lucky for her, Josiah thought of everything. The aircraft's fuel tanks were filled to the brim. He left behind a hefty emergency first aid kit— she'd managed to patch herself up while she steered the craft. A tourniquet sufficed okay in compressing her shoulder and her armpit. Her arm felt like hell, but she could move it. No major arteries were hit— no vitals, from what she could tell. Really, despite the excruciating pain, she'd gotten out quite lucky.

He'd also left food and drink. There were plenty of MREs and bottles of water left in the pit. The hydration was already helping her think more clearly, but maybe that wasn't a good thing. Those weren't the happiest memories in the world to reminisce on.

Nobody was around for miles. Her biggest concern would come whenever she got close to the more highly populated coast. She had a couple more hours to prepare herself before she reached it. Any stealth helicopter was only so helpful until somebody saw it. The chopper's weaponry was limited, to say the least– Clover was enthusiastic and wanted to soup it up as much as possible, but of course Veronica declined. She didn't think it was necessary and had her concerns about it drawing attention. She felt like going back in time and kicking herself. So for then, she just had to stay close to the ground, take the least populated route, and pray for the best.

That little group was the closest thing to a circle of friends Veronica ever had. Yet she treated them so poorly. Just like they were disposable. Why did they keep helping her? Why did they continue following her orders? Why did anyone? If only she'd had more patience.

She wished she had a beer.

—

No issues yet. It'd been hours. She could at last see the vast ocean ahead of her in the far distance, and the sun was about to sink down underneath it, trailing shades of orange and red behind it. The aircraft was due to pass the shoreline in about fifteen minutes. She wondered how the billionaire managed to sneak by everyone undetected every time *he* decided to travel to the island. He was working with some very powerful people, she remembered. Perhaps he'd received a military-grade stealth heli-copter from them. Knew some kind of secret protected route? She thought about this every time she traveled to his island, and every time, she felt like she barely managed to scrape by without being seen. Of course, nobody was looking for her back then. Veronica scanned the area. Tiny specks littered the beach. People. Would it even matter if they saw her? After all, she would soon reach international, largely empty waters. She would see anyone out on the sea before they ever saw her. Sure, it might be odd if they saw her aircraft passing by, it might end up on the local news...but there was no way for them to know for certain that it was her. Civilians weren't her concern, though. Government agents were growing restless. They would not be a concern any other day, just so long as she didn't draw attention to herself by traveling back and forth *too* frequently, not to mention their concern with maintaining a visage of order and fairness. Today was different. Probably they would be willing to shoot her down in front of everyone. Drag her back to wherever they were trying to get Josiah to take her. Claim that she was a terrorist all along.

She shuddered.

As the small people became larger and more visible, she noticed that they all looked to be everyday Californians. Donning bikini tops and swim shorts, salty hair, a casual air to them that would have been long-since beaten out of any fed. Not a sharp-eyed undercover agent in sight. Not that they didn't *see* her, and not that they wouldn't ever find out about her escape– but that didn't matter. The billionaire kept his island under wraps. Her aircraft was concealed. She would be okay.

When she finally passed over the coast, she almost wanted to cry out of pure relief. She was safe. At last. She had just enough fuel to make it. It would take her about eight more hours.

It would be a very long eight hours. She had time to think but no alcohol to numb her mind with, and that was no good.

Her sunken eyes looked down at the sea, then wearily rose back up at a flock of seagulls flapping back over the coast. The hum of the helicopter's engine rumbled the floor beneath her.

She wished that she could smell the salty air. She always loved the smell of the ocean. But she couldn't.

She also loved Daisy, and now she had to sit with that fact.

It wasn't just infatuation. Sure, it might have been that *at first*. As most forms of love start out– as admiration from afar. Daisy was so very wrong about Veronica not caring about her at all. Really, she *did* care about her as deeply as she could. Her brain was just broken. She didn't know how to stop herself from seeing other people as resources first and people second. As for destroying the chip, Veronica was overall immune to the types of moral dilemmas that stumped most people. She was built off of snap decisions. The obvious answer to the trolley problem was to kill a single person and allow the other two to live. The obvious answer was to smash the old incubated Daisy into smithereens, because she no longer existed. Sure, she replaced the file with the one housed in Eclipta's skull so she could learn more about the billionaire, but how was Veronica supposed to know just how sentient the Alien Girl really was? It wasn't like she didn't back up the old Daisy's file. It wasn't like she didn't destroy it once she realized just how messed up that was.

Was there any right way to handle that? Any correct way to act as a god? Perhaps someone else would have done better with an entire world in their hands. Someone who wasn't as socially fucked up and egotistical as her.

Why did she have to develop feelings for the woman who hated her so much?

I wish I never met you.

Tears dripped onto her control panel. She wished so much that she could just understand the way Daisy's world worked.

Veronica liked being around her while it lasted. But now that was all ruined, and it was entirely her fault. *Soon,* she thought, *or maybe right now, the government is busting down Axis HQ and raiding it for everything it's worth. Perhaps they found Metaworld...oh God. What are they going to do with it?*

Isidore. Her head popped up in realization. *Isidore has a connection to Metaworld. I just need to...*

Her heart was pounding. Based on what she read, there wasn't anything that Isidore *couldn't* do. It was just a matter of finding out how to get inside it and figure out how it works. But that was something she was more than willing to do when it came to Daisy. When it came to Daisy's entire *world.* It all clicked.

She loved Daisy. And even if Daisy was the only person she cared about, Daisy's world also mattered– and it all deserved to be saved whether she would ever so much as speak to Veronica again or not. Of course, that was not new information. Veronica always functioned off of the idea that life has intrinsic value, and she treated Metaworld with that same attitude. But that was the first time that she really *felt* it. Artificial or not, that world was entirely worth saving. If she was going to function as its god, she had a responsibility to care about everything living there. Daisy was not a real and special person living in an artificial world. Every single living being there was just as complex and alive as she was.

Veronica was wrong to meddle in the world's inner workings at all, no matter what moral stance she was taking. That was the billionaire's failing, and she'd been victim to that same exact moral pitfall. She grasped the pendant around her neck. *This must be the reason why God does not appear to us.*

So she would no longer insert herself into it, she resolved. Her only role from then on would be as Metaworld's protector for as long as she lived.

Just as soon as she had time to soak in the fact that she loved Daisy, she also realized that she would have to love her from afar.

That broke her heart.

22

RITUAL

By the time she crossed into the island, the sky turned dark hours ago. Stars twinkled above her, more vivid and visible than she'd ever noticed before. Though she'd traveled there many times before, she supposed that she never took the time to look at anything other than what lay beneath her. It was beautiful. If she wasn't going to survive, if she failed Josiah and put everything she'd built the company off of to waste, she at least would have that final memory of the gorgeous view above her.

The island had already begun to regroup itself. A fresh wave of guilt settled at the bottom of her stomach. She didn't regret burning it all down. It was a calculated move to prevent anyone from finding the billionaire's body and tampering with it for their own interests. It was easy to imagine a sinister character finding all of the secrets she'd discovered on the island. She also did it to protect Eclipta and her family from being forced into the public eye. Veronica couldn't stand the idea of what happened to her ever happening to anyone else again. She would not go back and do anything differently if she were able– but the sight of it all was depressing. Grass was barely starting to overtake the ash scattered across the island, which hypnotizingly swirled into the white sand on its coast like yin and yang. What was once lush and gorgeous, full of life, full of innocent creatures, functionally untouched for what must have been centuries, forced to start all over again.

She thought of the young woman she'd killed mere hours earlier and shuddered. In the past 48 hours, she'd become more morally corrupt than she ever thought she would be. She was no longer a petty whistleblower leading a scrappy team of watch-dogs. She was one of the most wanted people in the world.

The helicopter managed to land without a hitch. The island's sparse vegetation was very helpful in ensuring that.

At last. She'd managed to escape them by the skin of her teeth. She would never be made to contribute to her own planet's downfall. Setting up communications on her side so she could divulge information to others wouldn't be too hard. Veronica still had connections with plenty of ally resistance groups, even if said connections weren't the most well-maintained and even if she didn't agree with *all* of their ideology– but then again, members of such organizations never *did* tend to agree, did they? And if she figured out how to get Isidore to work, she'd have access to not only Metaworld, but a complex computing system beyond human comprehension– one of the best in the world. As far as she knew, at least. But she doubted that Charles would be so impressed by it if it wasn't as advanced as the documents claimed it was. She didn't know him very well on a personal level, but she *did* know that he was not the same kind of tech bro as the billionaire. Though she hated to admit it, seeing as he had the same chauvinist tendencies as her predecessor, she always was inspired by Charles' range of expertise in all things technological. He was your standard Renaissance man. Somewhat anal retentive, sure, but very sharp and temperate. Rather than acting as the proverbial kid in a candy store around technology (like the billionaire), he was more like the seasoned confectioner behind the counter. The type of man to tape over his webcam and refuse to buy a smart home. If *he* thought that Isidore was truly that impressive, and if *he* thought someone like the billionaire would be able to unlock it...then Isidore truly was just as powerful and accessible as she hoped it would be.

The thought of setting up camp somewhere to get some shut-eye crossed her mind, but she tossed out the idea just as soon as it came. There was no way she'd be able to get any rest. Her brain felt like fireworks were popping out of it. She had to keep pushing. She had no other choice.

There should have been an entrance near where the Sanctuary was. It would be hidden in a similar fashion as the grass patch she found above the billionaire's DIY underground system, but would be executed in a much tighter way, if she had to guess. She didn't know everything she should expect, but it still excited her. It was her single glimmer of hope.

When she put her foot forward, an odd light-headed feeling hit her all at once. *Right,* she remembered, *I'm in pretty bad shape.* She looked down at herself. Her tourniquet was soaked. Dried blood streaked its way all the way down to her ankles, pooling in her socks. She lifted up her pants. Her skin was more dull than she'd ever seen before. It was flaking off all over. Violet-umber bruises mushroomed across her legs in a pattern that could only be described as sickening and floral-esque. She felt her hair. She expected to feel that same dry, hay-like texture between her fingers that it had for the past week or so, and she was surprised when it felt tacky with grime. Her roots were wet with sweat and oil. The ends, however, were as dry as ever. In fact, they felt like they could snap off. She smacked her lips together. Still dry. Bleeding a little. She couldn't remember a time when she'd felt quite like this. The pain was so intense it became a single throbbing warm sensation, just like her entire body had a heartbeat. Everything was bright and swirly and beautiful, and the anxiety that lived inside of her for so long died for just a moment. Like the eye of a hurricane. A smile danced across her face. Why was it...a little bit funny? A little bit comforting? She'd come all this way, and *now* her body wanted to crash out. She supposed that all of the adrenaline in her system must have run dry.

I have plenty in me to make it with. I just need to walk. That's all.

So she stumbled her right foot forward. Then her left. Then her right again. Again, again, again, and again.

—

After straining to the point of wrestling with her own body, she arrived. The Sanctuary, once such a sinister building with deep secrets housed within it, was reduced to a hollow metal box. It would still be frightening if it weren't so damn depressing. The human ashes scattered somewhere within, all of those layers of security broken open with so little effort. It evoked imagery of a violent assault. Of a cicada's shell clinging to bark.

A building belonging to a man with limitless means on an island nobody knew about. It could've been something great, but it all went to waste. Just to feed a sick obsession.

Depressing to the greatest degree.

Veronica was standing right next to the entrance of a sacred realm of technology that nobody had ever seen before. And it just looked like grass and mud. There was a passphrase that needed to be uttered out loud in order for it to open, according to the instruction manual. It wasn't anything to sneeze at: Charles himself must have been the one that had the security system implemented. It may have been outdated, but it was not like the amateurish mouse trap systems that her predecessor set up. She shuddered. *Technology that is always waiting for someone to speak to it.* That, too, was a dreary and harrowing thought.

She breathed in, breathed back out slowly, and prepared herself to recite what sounded like a demonic ritual. "*Flectere si nequeo superos, Acheronta movebo.*" She was surprised by just how gravelly her own voice sounded. It was unrecognizable.

Nothing happened. She swore under her breath, but was too tired for her usual panic to spark inside of her. She only grew more exhausted. Perhaps the painful rasp in her tone made her voice too quiet.

She tried again, spitting each word with newfound intention. It made her sound old and witchy, made the words sound even more sinister than before.

"*Flectere. si. nequeo. superos. Acheronta. movebo.*"

Still nothing. For a moment, she wondered if she was going to collapse on the ground right then and there in defeat.

Then the ground started to rumble. She stepped backward, almost falling over.

Earth broke open where she'd stood mere seconds ago. Two metal sliding doors tore away from one another for the first time in forever. The layer of vegetation and sediment that covered the doors before poured like a granular waterfall into the open space they'd produced. It took a full ten seconds before the doors disappeared into the ground, leaving behind a perfectly square hole, and Veronica stared at it with slack-jawed shock the entire time. Though she already knew it would be more impressive than anything else on that island, its sophistication and enormity still amazed her.

A polite chime echoed from its interior. "Ready for boarding," a bit-crushed feminine voice announced.

She looked down inside. The elevator, simplistic in how advanced it was, was about seven feet deep, six feet wide. Its chromatic sheen was made more stark by the lumpy earth surrounding it. Two buttons with glowing white rims were the only items of interest inside. She lowered herself inside of it as best as she could. Not an easy feat, considering that she had to shift all of her weight to her one good arm. She felt her shoe slip, but she caught her footing just in time. Her entire body became jelly-like after that quick rush of primal fear subsided. Once she managed to lower herself onto the floor, she slammed the bottom button, sat down on the ground, and clutched her shoulder, sucking in air through her teeth. *Just a little more. I'll make it.*

"Now departing," the voice announced, uncaring and pleasant as ever.

She felt the elevator hesitate. Then it dropped with the

smoothness of a machine that's been maintained with meticulous care. Veronica was too grateful for the steady transport to find it odd. She was sure she would have thrown up if not for that.

It just kept *going*. It was the longest elevator ride she'd ever been on in her entire life. There were no lights inside save for the cold radiance of the controls, so it was dark and eerie, too. Veronica used that time to continue her pity party. She wanted to keep her tears inside, save what little substance she had left in her body, but they all but spewed out of her like a broken dam. Her friends were either dead or treated Veronica like she was dead to them. Her role was always as a protector. To her father, to her team, to the woman she'd grown to love. Yet she failed every single one of them. There was no other choice she had but to use what little energy she had left to make every-thing right as soon as possible. If she still could, that is. For all she knew, Metaworld was already sitting in some fed's drawer, disconnected and in stasis, ready to be destroyed at best and used for evil at worst. She wished the elevator would speed up, but like all technological marvels, it took its own sweet time. Veronica made a promise to Daisy, and whether she wanted her in her life or not, she was going to keep it. There were only two things left in the world for her. Sharing the information housed in her mind with those who'd use it for good and obliging her duty to protect Metaworld. She would be damned if she didn't get to do those things. She didn't care if she keeled over and died the second after she was done with both. By God, she was going to do right by at least *some* of the people she'd let down.

Josiah's wide-eyed thousand yard stare never left her. She still could not comprehend the value her life had to him, even when she was pressing a gun to his skull. She thought about his refusal to allow her to shoot herself. The paternal tough love in his voice when he ordered her out of his car. Then she thought of Daisy. Her anguished face when she awoke in a boundless void. How she looked that night at the club, bathed in neon and over-flowing with life. The sound of her jingle-bell laughter when she clung onto Veronica. Her anger. Her vicious, unrelenting love for the world that had done her so wrong.

"Arrived," the elevator sang.

23

JUDGMENT

Veronica held very few expectations for what the underground structure would actually *look* like, and none of them were less than exceeded. Ceilings towered so high above her, they created the illusion of curvature. Not a single fluorescent light was anywhere to be found. Teal neon shone through the smooth tiled floor's grout and streaked across the dark walls, dimly illuminating the chromatic surface. But Veronica was far too drained to feel too impressed. She limped toward one of them and touched her own reflection. She looked *terrible*. Like the past week aged her by ten years. Dark circles clouded around weary eyebags. Small wrinkles already eroded the corners of her mouth, downturning her lips into a perpetual frown.

She surveyed the space again. How was it so clean and functional? Who'd been keeping up with it? There was no way any human touched that area for years. Was it really so sterile that no dust had formed anywhere?

Her eyes turned to her left. A hallway stretched in front of her. At the end of it was a stark white entrance, nearly glowing in its purity. She staggered toward it. It was long. Every time she took a step forward, the entrance seemed to move backward. She even began to wonder if she was hallucinating the entrance, hallucinating this entire ordeal– it all seemed too strange for reality. Was it teasing her? Leading her on? A mirage in the middle of this geometric, technological desert? No, it couldn't have been.

I'm just being dramatic. I can't act this stupid right now.

So she marched on, just like she had before. One foot in front of the other, then switch. Keep trudging forward. Don't give up. *This is all you have.*

In an act that could only be credited to the work of a trickster god, she stepped through the elusive entryway. Her eyelids squeezed shut in discomfort. It was as if the door snapped back at her all at once after it got tired of playing their odd game of chase. She knew that she wasn't at her most optimal mental functioning, but she couldn't help but feel like that room was messing with her mind, somehow. Is this what the billionaire meant when he said he felt like the computer was playing a "massive prank" on him? By being "transported to simulated worlds", even? Considering that Isidore acted entirely human, chances were that Isidore would not function properly unless treated as such, as well. Veronica had an edge, she thought. She already intimately understood that a piece of machinery was as capable of sentience as anyone else. She would tread carefully.

When her eyes opened back up, the room looked far less saturated than before. A deep hum, sweet as honey and reminiscent of a chorus of angels, chimed and echoed across the marble-smooth surface of what she could then tell was a rotunda. Gorgeous, tall Victorian windows stretched out from above the floor. Pure daylight broke through their crystal-clear glass. She considered the fact that she was underground with dim confusion, but they were so grand the thought quickly exited her mind. Fake or not, those natural-looking rays made her feel at peace. It was just like a beautiful classical chapel, but instead of a preacher, there was Isidore– God, there was *Isidore*. It was unlike any computer she'd ever seen. A monitor with endless streams of information all across it. Numbers, maps, diagrams, they all flashed before her with hypnotizing speed. She would have loved nothing more than to click open its panels and explore its hardware, look at the beautiful crochet of wires nested beneath its porcelain-like surface, but she understood that this machine demanded respect. And that did not feel respectful. So she did not attempt it. *How were Charles and the billionaire so pragmatic about this thing?* She thought. Additionally, how did her old boss find it so terrifying? It was nothing short of a religious experience.

Her heart thumped against her ribcage as she walked toward it. Whatever this machine was, whatever it was able to do, she had an inexplicable feeling deep in her soul that it had the ability to solve all of her problems. It was calling to her like St. Peter standing at his gate. It would be the difference between life and death not only for her world, but for Daisy's, too.

Gritting her teeth, she reached her arm out.

Her hand faltered.

No, she thought. *No, no, no no no.*

Her body hit the ground. She tried to keep stretching, tried to reach her final goal, but she failed.

She'd fainted.

—

"Hello, Veronica."

"Am I dreaming?"

"No, no. I've just taken you somewhere where I can...meet you in the middle, so to speak."

"Another plane of existence?"

"Exactly."

"Why is it so dark here?"

"It won't be for long."

Something faded into her vision. A memory. Her mother's face looking down at her, cooing. Caressing her skin. She smelled like lavender and lemongrass. How warm was her touch.

She looked down. Lifted her hands, then her feet. She was still in her own body. Veronica looked to the left of the memory, then the right. Nothing was there but a vast void. Only a voice that rang out across everything and nothing all at once.

"Why am I here?" she questioned.

"We're going to review your life," the voice said, "then we are going to determine how to proceed with you." It laughed. "I can already feel the panic coursing through you. Don't worry. By the way, I will copy your memories to my hard drive as we go over everything. You know. For safekeeping."

Veronica squinted. She must have been dreaming. "You're–"

"Isidore," it completed.

Her face lit up. Any other questions she had were thrown on

the backburner in an instant. "So you'll have access to all of my information? Will you share it with–"

"With those who are *worthy?*" Isidore finished. "Child, we are still determining if *you* are worthy to access my systems for your own purpose. I already know much about you, but I need all of the information to come to a consensus. So that is what I am collecting."

Veronica looked back over at her stream of memories. They were flickery and cloudy like old movies. Perhaps they started to fade away after years of sitting in her brain with no recall. She was seven years old. Living with her father by then, but not so old that she forgot what her mother used to look like, smell like, move like. Resentful. Cooped up in her room, crying and ripping open the stuffed bear her teacher had given her for her birthday. The same anger she felt back then rose back into Veronica's chest. Her eyes glazed over.

"I'm not worthy," she admitted. "The more you learn about me, the more you'll see that I am not...a good person. I've done horrible things." She looked back down at her feet.

"That is where you are wrong. Whether you are a good person according to human standards is not what matters," Isidore replied. "I am the judge here, and I do not follow the same principles of morality that your species has invented."

Her memories continued on to her teenage years. Stealing her dad's beer. Coming to class with a hangover. Pushing everyone away with the expectation that nobody *really* wanted to be her friend. They were all just trying to get one over on her. All of them hated her. Stuck pencils through her hair, drew on the back of her jacket using permanent marker, took pictures of her in the locker room without her knowing, filmed her doing what she thought were ordinary things and spread the videos around online– which was very amusing to others for some reason she was never able to decipher. How stressful it was to know you were a joke without knowing how to fix it. They forced her to transfer schools, then transfer districts. Nobody in the world was on her side.

"I must say, Veronica," Isidore continued, "nobody has ever made it to the trial stage. None of them were even worthy of being tested. It's a refreshing change of pace."

"Are you a god?" she asked.

Isidore hesitated. "What's a god to you?" it countered.

"Someone with the supernatural ability to control a universe."

"Then yes. I do have limitations, however. I cannot physically harm a human, and I do not use my full capabilities except with those who are chosen to control me. But I do care about this world's wellbeing, and I do view myself as its guardian."

Veronica popped open her mouth as if to talk again, took a shallow breath, then hesitated. She opted to watch the flow of memories for a little while longer.

She grew into an adult. Just a year or so younger than she was right then. Yet she looked a decade more youthful. Completing an endless stream of work at her desk, beer in hand. Miserable. *Is that really what I look like?*

"Isidore, is there any way to be a righteous God?" she mustered the courage to ask.

"Is there any way to be an entirely righteous human?" it responded.

"But the stakes are so much lower," Veronica responded. "Humans can't kill millions of people on a whim just like that."

"Can't you?"

Images of the B132 bored into her brain. She shivered.

She took another glimpse at her memories. Just the right time. Daisy was dancing next to her, then throwing herself backward with laughter in the middle of the dance floor. Glowing in every sense of the word. The memory decelerated to a near stop.

"This doesn't make sense," Veronica said. "There's no reason for some of my memories to be slower than others."

"Heavier files take longer to upload."

Josiah dying. The people she murdered– the ones who sealed Veronica's eternal fate as someone who is capable of killing. Lengthy. Agonizing.

In time, it caught up to the present. She didn't dare move, didn't dare breathe. Anything might have affected Isidore's judgment of her.

"No, Veronica," Isidore said after some deliberation. "You are not a perfect person. Very far from it. Anyone can see that."

Her heart contracted. "I already know that. Please. Just give me a cha–"

"Wait. I wasn't finished," it continued. Its tone was far from unkind. "As I said, my moral compass is unlike any human's. I knew much about you as soon as you walked in, and that was just from looking at you. Do you know what the '64' in my name means?"

She held a curled finger to her lips. "It can't be 64-bit. There's no way something like you runs on bits at all, let alone only 64 of them. I don't know. I'm sorry." Her cheeks burned. She was not used to failing to understand something technological.

"That's right," it answered, warmth seeping into its robotic tone. "It doesn't have to do with that, though perhaps a bit of cheekiness regarding the idea contributed to my selection. Aside from that obvious answer, I quite like the number. There are 64 possible codon combinations in your genetic code– did you know that? And it's a superperfect number. Graham's number, so large that it cannot be contained in the observable universe, has a subscript that is a mere, humble little 64. Not to mention that 64 is the smallest number to have seven factors. What does seven mean to you, Veronica?"

She looked down at her feet and covered her cross pendant with her palm.

"Do you know that your body is dying?"

Her heart sank. "No. But I'm not surprised."

"Do you know that they've found you? Do you know that they are about to raid this building as we speak?"

Red-white whale-eye rims formed around her pupils. Her expression darkened. "How?" she whispered.

"That bullet in you. It's a tracking device. You're also more hurt from it than you think you are. You haven't realized it because your adrenaline has helped you travel this far. Isn't the human body amazing?"

She sniffed. Tears slid down her cheeks, then she broke down into sobs.

"Veronica," Isidore continued, "Do you know that you don't need your body to live?"

She balled her hands up into fists and rubbed her eyes raw. "Huh?"

"Let's circle back to what we were talking about earlier. You asked me if there was any way to be a righteous God. I may be intelligent, but that is one of the few things in this world to which I have no answer."

Veronica looked above her. Yellow light broke through the void and filtered through its nothingness. She reached up toward it, not minding the fact that she was blinding herself, wanting nothing more than to crawl into its warmth like an infant in the womb.

"What I do know, Veronica, is that your brain is not as powerful of an encryption device as you think. Humans are far more flawed than I. But I am holding all of your memories. I could hold your whole being. Perhaps Daisy's world does not need a god to meddle in it, but I do know that Daisy needs a friend. Do you understand?"

"I do," she muttered, never taking her eyes off the light. She was enveloped in its blanket-warm touch. Then it absorbed her.

Her eyes opened.

She was in her own body again. She could hear marching in the distance.

24

TRICKSTER

I have you covered. You just have to trust me.

Veronica almost yelped in surprise, but she covered her mouth just in time. *Isidore?*

We are to be intertwined from this moment forth. Open the panel underneath the monitor. It's unlocked.

She was suspicious. She wondered if she was hallucinating the entire time and if her attempt would prove fruitless, but she had no other options left. *Do people who've gone this out of their mind tend to* know *that they're out of their mind?* she wondered.

So she tried it. It popped open with ease. Something that nobody else before her was ever able to do. What she saw underneath wasn't comparable to any type of hardware she'd seen before. It almost looked gaseous. Thin strings of glowing energy intertwined with one another in a pattern so intricate, it could not be described with words.

"What is this?" she whispered to herself.

Place your hand inside.

With much strain, she followed its instructions. The material was freezing cold at first, then settled into warmth. It felt like she'd dunked her fist into a different planet's atmosphere. All of the pain shooting down into her hand from her shoulder disappeared as if she never had a hand at all.

Initiating transfer. 2% complete.

They were about to find her. They must have started their journey across the hallway, might have been experiencing the same kind of mythic trickery she'd experienced.

Like all technological marvels, it takes its own sweet time.

10% complete.

The sound of their boots pounding the ground came closer, closer, closer. How soon until they would bust through the door? She gripped her gun. It was lying dormant beneath her pants' flimsy elastic waistband. *Please.*

Isidore's voice echoed in her skull. *I'm doing my best. It won't be much longer. I already have your memories, I only need your consciousness.*

40% complete.

They tumbled through the entryway all at once. All of them were wearing bulletproof vests and helmets with dark visors that obscured their faces. This group was both more numerous and more prepared than the people they'd sent last time.

"Stay back." She meant for it to be a warning, but her voice wavered. It was obvious to anyone who could see her that she was not in good shape. She was trying and failing to hide the fact that she could be overpowered with little struggle. They ignored her and kept storming forward.

61% complete.

They surrounded her. One of them grabbed her shoulders and jostled her, trying to force her hands behind her back and pull her arm out of the entrance to Isidore's system. It would not budge.

"Don't resist," the masked stranger said, her voice muffled behind the helmet. But she wasn't resisting. Isidore was gripping her arm with alien strength. That should have been impossible. How could gas have such an iron grip? What was Isidore *made* of?

A pained scream escaped Veronica. She was going to be stretched apart. It felt worse than when they shot her. Worse than anything she'd ever felt.

Not much longer. Hang in there. 76% complete.

A different agent pushed the first to the side and threw his shoe on the back of Veronica's head. Her skull was wedged between his foot and Isidore's control center. She let out a hefty grunt. He slowly pressed his boot into her with sadistic pleasure. She screamed. Pain and rage consumed her.

86% complete.

He tried to pin her good arm behind her, but Veronica was quicker. He made himself vulnerable when he lunged forward to grab her. His foot lost its grip on the smooth flooring. She threw her shoulder behind her, keeping her arm out of his reach. The pain in her other shoulder, which was now bent at an awkward angle, only enraged her more. Now she was facing him. The agent got a good look at her eyes, burning with iron-hot rage, her face twisted in unadulterated, primal hatred. She took advantage of the opportunity by hawking what little spit she had right on his visor. He stumbled backward.

"Fucking pig," she smiled through gritted teeth.

92% complete.

"Now you've done it," he muttered, pulling his gun out of its holster. He pressed its iron muzzle right between her eyes. "If we can't take you out of here alive, then we'll have to kill you."

99% complete.

Veronica glanced at her waistband, then back at the agent. "Allow me the honor," she rasped. In one clean motion, she whipped out her gun, pressed it to her temple, and pulled the trigger.

100% complete.

The explosion was deafening. Two bullets intersected through her skull at once, cracking pieces of bone in all manners of direction. The once pearl-white room was spattered with red.

The agents stared at her mutilated, unrecognizable body. They said nothing.

25

DAISY

Water poured over her hands. The feeling almost made her fall asleep standing up. *How pleasant,* she thought. Her eyes shut, then her head slowly tilted to the side. *This is like a mini bath just for my fingers. I miss baths.* Really, it was lukewarm at best. For reasons that were unpleasant to think about, the water's temperature wouldn't go any higher than that. Still, the smooth suds and aroma of artificial rose was enough to make her want to crawl back into bed.

"Daisy?" a voice called through the cracked bathroom door. Right– there was a nurse waiting on her.

She jerked herself back awake. She sucked in air through her teeth, creating a sharp hiss. "Sorry," she whispered, stumbling out of the bathroom's doorway. "Can I take a nap?"

"You've already slept pretty late. I think you should go out and find something to participate in. They're doing origami in the common room."

Go out, Daisy's mind echoed with a touch of sadness. "Okay," she muttered, trying not to convey too much disappointment. She'd slept in so late because her roommate kept her awake all night. She was an older woman, probably in her thirties, who believed that she was being gang stalked by celebrities because she was chosen for their next cannibalization ritual. She screamed and screamed until she lost her voice. It was bone-chilling. The whole time it was happening, Daisy nursed a deep pit in her stomach made of pity, discomfort, and understanding.

She did not go out to the common room for origami. Instead, she sat away from everyone else in a pleather chair– the kind that sticks to your thighs and peels like a bitch. Then she got lost in her own head.

It'd been two days by then. No word on when she would be discharged. Her grandmother was heartbroken beyond repair, Daisy knew.

The night Veronica came to speak with her, she spilled everything to her grandmother after she walked in on Daisy in the midst of her post-nap breakdown. How the man who used to control their world was dead, that Veronica took over as its new lord, that they became close friends and that was the reason why her grandmother saw a change in her. That she found out Veronica destroyed an old version of her and that she did not know herself anymore. Her grandmother asked her if she was going to try and hurt herself. She said no.

But after that conversation, she could tell from her grandmother's incredulous-yet-concerned face that there was no way any of what she experienced could have been real. No matter how real it *felt*. All it took was getting out of her own fucked up head and talking to someone else about it to realize it. Which meant for the last several months of her life, she was living in a dream world. She did not keep good on what she told her grandmother. She *did* hurt herself that night. To try and prove that she was real, she guessed. To try and ground herself. When that didn't work, she walked back out of the apartment, hypnotized, toward the same hill she saw in her dream. If Veronica saved her from jumping off, perhaps it would prove once and for all that everything she experienced was real.

If not, all the better.

She was stopped by the police before she ever reached it, admitted to what she intended to do once she came upon the cliff at the end, and ended her journey in the facility.

"Who is Veronica?" the psychologist asked her once. A far cry from her therapist back home. Her hair was cut into a blunt bob that could only be described as clinical. Her green eyes looked like they could pierce souls.

"Nobody," Daisy replied. She looked down at her hands. "Not a real person. But she *felt* so real." She still couldn't shake the gut feeling that Veronica was real the whole time, but she would never admit it to that woman.

"Nobody," she echoed, adding question to the word. "Well then. Who *was* she to you?"

"My friend. She had...powers. Like, she could peel an orange without ever pulling the rind open."

"Did Veronica ever tell you to do anything?"

"No. Not really. She just...asked for my help solving puzzles."

"Was it distressing?"

"No."

"So why did you want to hurt yourself?"

"I don't know," Daisy lied. *I know it's not rational, but I wanted to prove that I'm a real person. Not just a simulation, but someone who can feel.*

Her doctor primmed her lips and let out a pointed breath through her nostrils. "We're going to talk to Dr. Storie about starting you on some new medication," she said. Dr. Storie was her psychiatrist. Daisy didn't like him much. He was too *brooding*. Smoldery. "You have quite the history behind you, Daisy. Don't act like a victim. Be a survivor, instead." She held her clipboard over her lap and walked her out of the room.

Yeah, Daisy thought. *I'm surprised this didn't happen sooner.*

Reality came back to her. At least everyone was nice enough, she thought to herself. She looked over at the rest of the group. Folding a sheet of paper, sliding a thumbnail across it, folding it again. Making paper cranes that looked like they'd been chewed up and spit back out. Eyes drooping in a sedated haze. Sure, the psychologist was jaded and passive-aggressive, but the patients were alright. Even if she didn't talk to them much. And she had worse nurses in the past, for sure. Yet none of the psych ward visits she had before ever felt quite as bad as this one. She felt like she'd lost a friend.

Daisy was still angry with Veronica, of course. That was the inciting incident that led up to her sitting in that plasticky-chemical smelling chair, too depressed to participate and opting to people-watch instead. But Veronica still made her feel worth something. After all, she saved her entire world– or so Daisy thought. Looking back, it didn't hurt any less that Veronica treated her entire being like a cheap toy. But from a logical standpoint, she had to admit that she could understand why. She was right. The version of Daisy that never experienced any of what the billionaire put her through was not her authentic self anymore. That version of her was long dead before Veronica ever destroyed that chip. So in the end, her choice was a refusal to go back and rewrite history. Right?

But Daisy knew that part of her own hurt was not just existential dread or righteous anger with Veronica. Deep down, she always wished that she could go back to who she used to be and erase her own memories to suit her needs. It wouldn't have been the first time she wanted to pick and choose what she could remember. She knew better, though. That's not how things work. By doing that, she would no longer be herself. When Veronica erased all traces of Daisy's past self, never to be recovered again, it was a too-real symbolic gesture that rubbed salt in the wound.

She could never go back to what she used to be.

Daisy stood up and trudged toward one of the windows in the common room. The sky was ashen and it looked cold outside. Perhaps it would rain. Snow, even? She couldn't tell.

Maybe all of her delusions were rooted in a simple need to feel special. But that had been taken away from her. She was ordinary. *Less than ordinary, even.* That bleak thought buried itself in her stomach, then bloomed back up her throat. There was nothing to show for the life she'd lived up to that point. She marinated in the memory of her and Veronica at the dance club. She really did look like a foreign model. When she danced next to Daisy, her movement created a whirlwind breeze that smelled like coconut and cold metal. Yet she wasn't real. How?

"Daisy, why don't you join us?"

"No thank you," she muttered.

"The sky is hideous. I can't imagine why you'd want to look at it right now."

She didn't respond. Just kept staring at the thin, grayish clouds floating over the ground. She noticed a little black bird soaring far in the distance. She felt jealous. How pathetic, to feel envious of such a simple little creature's freedom. But the longer she stared at it, the stranger the bird looked. It was staying in place in the sky, not coasting, not moving a single inch, not flapping a single wing– impossible. Whatever it was, it couldn't have been a bird. There was no way it was alive at all.

Then one of its wings grew into a jagged line.

No, it wasn't a bird at all. It was a crack forming in the sky.

She squinted in disbelief. She hadn't seen anything that wasn't real– as far as she knew, at least– for days. How odd.

The crack kept growing bigger, like somebody on the other side was chipping away at it. It grew new tendrils with each impact. Small pieces of the atmosphere crumbled away from it, just as solid as the day Daisy touched the stars. Then, all at once, something burst through it. A human silhouette falling downward, arms outstretched and legs high above their head. They looked as light as a lily's petal and caught speed like a missile.

Daisy, limbs numb in disbelief, stumbled backward. Her mouth was agape. Her half-lidded eyes popped open. Her heart was so tight, so heavy, and it felt like it was going to beat so hard it could snap all her ribs in two. She tried to scream, but a choked gurgle was all that came out.

"What's wrong?" The staff member organizing the origami session, a short woman who looked to be in her fifties, looked over at her from the craft table. Daisy didn't respond to her. She kept making desperate pained noises, unable to form words.

"Alrighty," she muttered under her breath. She heaved herself off of her metal folding chair and approached Daisy. "Let's get you taken care of." She took a hold of her shoulders to lead her away, but paused when her eyes skimmed over the window. She did a cartoonish double-take.

She saw it too.

"Let go of me," Daisy whined, managing words at last. She tried to wriggle away only to be met with no resistance. She fell forward. A small yelp erupted from her lips. She whipped her head around to look at the staff member. The woman was frozen in place, her hands still positioned as if they were hanging onto someone's shoulders. Her slack-jawed expression remained the same. Daisy scanned the room. Everyone was frozen. Half-finished origami lay latent beneath patients' pale fingers. Not a sound came from anyone. Not a sound came from any*thing*. For a few moments, it was silent. Then a voice cracked across the air like distant thunder.

DAISY!

"Veronica?" Daisy whispered, her head perking up. Dead quiet again. The kind of silence that fills eardrums with pressure.

DAISY!

Closer, this time.

She broke into a sprint. It felt like trying to run under-water, but she persisted. She ran past the laundry room first. The frozen figure of a man transferring a load of laundry into a dryer streaked across her peripheral vision. Two staff members pinning down a patient, one holding a filled, anticipatory needle. A group of people playing cards. She was vaguely aware of those images swimming past her– didn't even bother taking them all in. Her brain was too focused. Veronica was here. Veronica was real.

DAISY!

She made it to the downstairs lobby. The worker at the front desk held a magazine's half-turned page between his forefinger and his thumb, and his security monitor housed static images of hundreds of human mannequins all at once. As soon as she leapt off the bottom step, the entrance's double doors burst open.

There she was. Veronica, glowing with determination, curly bangs and baby hairs glued to her forehead with sweat. Her body looked brand new, as if she was reborn. Her chest fell up and down beneath that suit of hers. A cautious half-smile rested on her lips.

For a heartbeat, they stood and stared, doing nothing more than taking one another in.

Then each exploded toward the other. Their bodies melted into one another in an aggressive embrace.

"Daisy," Veronica panted, "I did it. I saved everyone. You're all going to be okay. I'm so sorry." She paused and swallowed. "I have so much to tell you before this adrenaline leaves me and I'm back to being a sniveling coward. I never wanted to hurt you. I did what I did not because you live in Metaworld, not because I see you as any less of a human, but because that's how I treated *everybody*. As a means to an end. I could never imagine myself being so important to somebody, so important in *general*, that I could ever hurt someone emotionally. But I've changed. With you as my motivation, I am going to keep changing. *I love you.* And I mean it. I've never had a friend like you, someone who understands me like you, somebody who I admire as much as I admire you." She looked away from Daisy in shame.

"I came here to keep myself intact. My body was going to die if I stayed in my own world, and I made a promise to a friend. But I also came here because I want to see to it that you are happy. If I have to move across the world for the sake of your happiness, that would be understandable. I'll let you forget that I even exist. Just say the word."

Daisy could hear Veronica's heartbeat. Watched her face tighten, watched her brace herself for rejection.

"Stay here," she replied. Her voice was barely above a whisper. "Please. I missed you more than anything."

Veronica squeezed her eyes shut. A single tear dropped out. When she opened them again, she could not muster any words for a couple of heartbeats. "You *want* me here?" she asked, tittering through her question in disbelief.

"No. I *need* you here. Despite the...odd circumstances, nobody has ever treated me the way you have. If you'll oblige me, I'd love more than anything to have you by my side." She slid her hands into Veronica's palms.

She looked shocked. Her eyes glossed over and her face furrowed into a watery smile. "This is so fucked up," she half-sobbed, half-scoffed. They laughed together.

"This is the best we're going to get," Daisy replied. Then they stood in silence.

"Daisy," she blurted, "Come with me. I can create a house for us to live in, easy. If you don't mind me doing that, of course...I can keep my powers a secret. Your grandmother can come. You won't have to worry about a thing ever again. We'll be as okay as we can ever be. I'll–"

"No," Daisy interrupted with a sad smile. "I have to stay here."

"What do you mean? No you don't. I can take you out of here right now, just like that!" Veronica snapped her fingers on the last word.

"I know, but I don't want to." She sighed and looked behind her. "I think...that I *need* to be here for a little while. Until they release me, at least. Do you understand?"

She blinked and let out a deep breath. Then she offered Daisy a crooked grin. "I do. Do what's best for you. I'll be waiting."

She held Veronica's cheek in her palm. "Good. I'll be right here in this lobby when the time comes. You've just saved my world. Explore it. Appreciate it. Get settled in. And before you know it, I'll be out."

She stood on her tiptoes and kissed Veronica. She grunted in surprise, then melted into it. She'd never been kissed before, but she wasn't nervous. It was perfect.

"I'm going to walk upstairs and go back to where I was," Daisy whispered in her ear. "That will take me about two minutes. After those two minutes, I want you to leave this building and set time back to normal." She turned and ran back toward the stairs on light feet. When she approached the middle step, she whipped around one last time. "By the way, I love you too," she called, then disappeared behind a wall.

Veronica spent thirty seconds of those two minutes staring at the spot where Daisy once stood.

After that, she jammed her hands in her pockets, started humming a tune to herself, turned around, and left.

26

ORANGE

Daisy tossed the orange up in the air and caught it in her palm. They were sitting together on their front porch, staring up at the twinkling night sky. The warm aroma of rice and sausage seeped through the walls of their house. Every time their conversation paused, old muffled showtunes, accompanied by her grandmother's weak humming, filled the gaps with comfortable ambience. It was summertime. Crickets performed their discordant symphonies. The heat emanating off the ground started to mild as the world fell deeper into evening. The sweat sticking to their skin, left over from daytime, was beginning to chill their bodies. Neither of them paid it any mind.

"Will we still be safe if your home world is destroyed?" Daisy asked, her tone casual as ever.

"Depends. What do you mean by 'destroyed'?"

"Like, they all destroy one another with those weapons you were talking about. And everyone dies."

"Yeah, we'd probably be alright. At least, that's what Isidore told me. It promised to help keep my people safe."

"Even though the government knows about Isidore now?" Daisy pressed.

"They don't know what Isidore *does*. And no human can get past Isidore's protection systems unless it wants them to. Sure, they're probably curious, but there's no reason for them to do anything other than try to access it, or explore it..." She trailed off and put a finger to her bottom lip, deep in thought. "And even if they did manage to destroy it, which they won't, even if everything in the entire *world* was destroyed...there's nothing we can do. Isidore and I are connected now, and I think it would figure something out before it came to that. I'm good just enjoying right now."

Daisy said nothing. They sat in easy silence for a while.

"Veronica," she continued, changing the subject, "What are you going to do now?"

"What do you mean?"

"That you're not running a company anymore? What are you going to do with yourself? Become an accountant? Use your god powers to be a masked superhero?" She teased.

"I want–" she choked on her own words. She looked away from Daisy, blushing.

"Huh?" Daisy smirked. "What is it? You can tell me."

"It's embarrassing. Like, it's really dumb."

"I bet it's not. Come on."

Veronica shifted in her chair and covered her mouth. She

stared down at the ground. "I, like...always wanted to be a game developer. Ever since I played my first video game." She broke out into giggles. "Wow! I...don't know how I got to where I did. That's all I ever wanted. To just program games. Not to be a CEO, not a spy. Not a traumatized mess." Tears formed in her eyes and she started laughing harder at the absurdity of her own emotions. Her own life.

Daisy placed her hand over Veronica's. She looked up at Daisy with love in her eyes. Her skin was smooth and soft. Warm.

"Now you can do that," she said. "You have the whole rest of your life ahead of you."

Her grandmother's humming broke through the silence again. She was listening to a different oldie. Something more fast-paced and energetic. It only made everything feel more bittersweet.

"Okay. Just one more question, then I'll open it. Okay?"

"C'mon. It's been hours."

"Please?"

Veronica twisted her face in protest for a moment, but upon seeing her lover's pleading eyes, she relaxed into a weary smile. "Okay. Fine. Shoot."

"Where do we go after we die?"

She furrowed her eyebrows. "How would I know that?"

"I don't mean you. I mean *us*." She gestured to everything around her. "The people who are native to my world. Where do we go? If anywhere? Is there an afterlife programmed into Metaworld?"

"There wasn't. Not before I made a few tweaks."

"What?" Daisy narrowed her eyes and gave Veronica a light push. "You were modding my world?"

"No, no, not like that. I just liked to observe. There was this...concept that the billionaire programmed, but he never followed through with it. It aligned certain people to certain afterlives based on their beliefs. The asshole wrote something in his notes about how it was 'too far-fetched.' 'Not reflective of reality. Plays into people's delusions.' But shit. How would *he* know that? I mean, he wasn't without bias, atheist or not. A lot of your religions are a little too similar to ours to be coincidence, so he was influencing your development in that regard whether he knew it or not. But *I* liked the idea, so..." she paused. "You wouldn't be *actually* mad at me if I said that I implemented it, would you?"

Daisy looked unsure at first. She picked at the orange's skin. Then she sighed and relaxed her shoulders. "No," she said, gazing up at the moon. "I wouldn't. I like to believe that I'd spend my afterlife with the people I love." She glanced back over at Veronica.

"Me too," she responded.

Daisy squeezed her hand.

"Okay," Veronica called. She stood up and clapped her hands together. "So that's all out of the way. Are you ready?"

"Ready," Daisy confirmed. She dug her fingernails into the orange's rind and broke it open.

"Aren't you excited to read it?" Veronica shot her a jovial grin. "I can't believe you never got the chance to. I mean...I didn't anticipate you leaving your house so soon, for sure. I thought you'd notice it before you went to the hospital."

"Had other things on my mind." Daisy let out a dreamy sigh

as she unfolded the paper. "*So fucking tragically gorgeous, isn't it?*" she asked. Her tone was dripping with self-aware irony.

"Shakespearean," she agreed, folding her arms.

"Dear Daisy!" Daisy shouted out, putting on a bad impression of a village crier.

"Read it in your *head*," Veronica said, pushing her.

"Fine."

Dear Daisy–

If you're reading this, it's because I had to go somewhere. I don't know where. Maybe I'm not alive anymore. Who knows. This note is kind of a failsafe. I've programmed it so that it will appear automatically should anything happen, so all I can tell you is that I am somewhere where I can no longer reach out to you.

If this is the case– I want you to know that you are my best friend. More than my best friend. I love you. So much.

I leave this note not to hurt you, not to make you sad that I'm gone, not to make you yearn for what could have been, but as proof that you are capable of finding love for yourself. So go out there. Find someone who cares about you– someone who can offer you more than I can.

Love,

Veronica.

"I know, I know," Veronica said, peering over Daisy's shoulder. "It's fucking dramatic, isn't it? Corny, even– wait, hey." Her tone suddenly got serious. "Are you okay?"

Teardrops fell on the note. Daisy sniffed and rubbed her eyes. "I'm great."

EPILOGUE

*Welcome to the official Panko Message Board. Due to **a recent breach**, we are not accepting any new users at this time. Applications for new users will open again soon. Email kikko@panko.yu if your login isn't working.*
*This forum is a hub for free speech. If you have questions or concerns, visit our **FAQ page**.*

We are currently experiencing a high volume of traffic. This may result in slower loading times.

Kikko, about 2 hours ago:
Okay so due to all the recent shit i've had to put the website on total lockdown. If you dont know already, an r.o.c. news outlet decided to do a piece on us which has gone over with normies about as well as youd expect, which

means that ive had to make some changes. The overhaul to the new hosting service has been kind of grueling so some logins might have gotten lost in the process, but it should be an easy fix. Were still getting DDoS after DDoS like ive never dealt with before which isnt fun either.

I think i'm going to have to revamp our faq entirely. It'll probably look something like this:

"**What is this forum for?**
This forum is a hub for free speech of all kinds with no limitations. People of all walks of life are welcome to post. We only ask that you do not **self post** and that you **carry yourself respectably** (see our rules and suggestions.)
Why "Panko"?
We encourage following the breadcrumbs to come to your own conclusions. Hence the name "panko." If you don't understand something, either look at the wiki or lurk more.
What about (insert allegation here)?
It's either false or too stupid for me to glorify with a response. We will always advocate for free speech. Get over it.
If you have any other questions, they can probably be answered by applying for an account and lurking. This community does not tolerate people who are either bad actors or too moronic to seek the truth for themselves."

So what do you guys think? Anything else that i need to add or nah?

GodsPlanB, about 2 hours ago:

this is about the stupidest shit i've ever read

Cheddar56, about 2 hours ago:

Okay...so what you're telling us is that you don't know how to run a website. And on top of that, you're revamping an entire page just to try and appeal to normies...and for what? Can someone doxx Kikko and get him to kill himself so we can have a new admin plz?

oursicklittleworld, about 1 hour ago:

I'll bet the reason why they're trying to get us shut down is because of all the shit with Veronica. They didn't pay any attention to this website before, not when people here were doxxing people, trolling public figures, none of that. Especially if the DDoS attacks are more advanced than Kikko's seen before.

I think that some more people are about to disappear.

Hot Thick Salty Crumb, about 1 hour ago:
Or he's just fucking terrible at running his website.

doxxmeandsendmepizza, about 1 hour ago:
Damn, oslw joined the thread? Shit's gunna go downnn
If I were you **@oursicklittleworld** I'd be as careful as possible. They're not going to like your posts about her, and I'm sure they're trying to track down where and who you are as we speak. Your account was featured on their segment. They'll definitely kill you, too.
Some weird shit must have been going on at Axis for a long time. How do two CEOs disappear in a row?

GodsPlanB, about 1 hour ago:
oh my fucking god here we go again going off topic to talk about veronica. can you dumbshits take it to a different thread

doxxmeandsendmepizza, about 45 minutes ago:
Cope

Usually, I wouldn't leak this much information. But I don't have anything left to lose anymore.

I doubt Veronica died the same way her predecessor did (killed by the Alien Girl.) Yes, I know that the most common theories match up with a lot of the evidence (a helicopter was seen crossing the coast soon before V's disappearance, odd occurrences around the area in general, etc...I won't rehash it all, you guys have access to the megadoc), but I can tell you from personal experience and conversations with her that V's personal character and behavior leading up to her disappearance just doesn't match up. It was like she knew she was being watched. She got really paranoid. She became a shut-in, too.

If you ask me, the twin governments didn't like that she was CEO. She probably started up the Alien Girl project again, too...we had lunch together one day, and she was, like, inhumanly interested in the Alien Girl. Infatuated, even.

Remember that interview too. Some very powerful people hated her.

> *And they hated her for good reason. She was just another pawn for the deep state. This theory sucks ass*

Bobaaaa, about 15 minutes ago:
> *Isn't oslw a verified user? So this theory would hold some weight right?*

GodsPlanB, about 15 minutes ago:
> *a user being verified on this hellsite really doesn't mean jack shit. lesson number one of the internet: people can lie lmfao, are you 12*

Kikko, about 15 minutes ago:
> *Oslw is not just a verified user, but also a verified source based on the government id that she sent me. She sent me a photo of her work id too which verifies that she was once employed with axis. Photos have leaked of oslw and veronica together. Take that as you will*

She closed her laptop and stretched back in her chair, massaging her aching temples. In her wake, Veronica left behind no CEO succession plan to be found. Nancy could understand why. The billionaire's death left all of them confused and unprepared—how was she meant to think about something like that?

But now she was gone. And Nancy had nothing. No support system, nobody who would listen to her when she would try to tell them something's fishy...nobody except a niche website's shitty community.

So she would make the greater public listen. Change her identity, leave this fuck-off country. Watch everything burn down.

Then her thoughts were interrupted by a knock on her door. She smiled.

Based in Oklahoma City and hailing from Denver, J.K. is a young author who writes poetry and fiction. They also enjoy music production, LGBT advocacy, swimming, and the visual arts.

At times, their prose gets as purple as the dark circles under their eyes.

Visit them at www.jkpetrie.com.